JEF

RED GIRL JUMPING

an experimental memoir written by memory

Kim Merrill

2026

Acknowledgements

Thank you to the writers and friends who read pages, gave notes, and encouraged me during the creation of this book:

Leo Carey, Laura Maria Censabella, Louise Crawford, Don Cummings, David Ferguson, Maria Iosifescu, Kathleen Kelly, Quincy Long, Mary Proenza, Virginia Reed, Susan Vitucci, Members of Ensemble Studio Theatre Playwrights Unit, The MacDowell Colony, Virginia Center for Creative Arts, and Helene Wurlitzer Foundation.

Red Girl Jumping
an experimental memoir written by memory

Copyright © 2026 Kim Merrill

Cover Art Copyright © 2026 Sadie M. Glas

ISBN 978-1-969885-01-3

ISSN 1084-547X

This is volume 108 of
The Journal of Experimental Fiction

JEF Books/Depth Charge Publishing
Arlington Heights, Illinois

"The Foremost in Innovative Fiction"
Experimentalfiction.com

RED GIRL JUMPING

an experimental memoir written by memory

Kim Merrill

Chapter 1
Falling

I hang like a fool in the sky.

Kimberly sits on a rock.

Today is her birthday. To celebrate she pushed a wheelbarrow up the hill. She set a stick on fire. She held the stick to piles of jumbled paper. Family letters. Journals. Photos of herself. She watches her journals burn and covers her mouth with her hand.

We flecks of ash fly high. Kimberly watches us float. Fifty years of life rise out of her lungs, out of her heart, out of her very cells as we dance freely, lightly, into an ether of new. She will be reborn. Released. Renewed. Healed!

What kind of idiot told her that?

I swoop to rise, release, fly off, until I start to fall. Other ashes pass me, waving as they zoom. I call to them for help. I strain my ashy wings. Still I can't rise up. Kimberly's walking down the hill, wheelbarrow bouncing empty, so I make a decision. Find the wind. I ride it down adrift, knowing I'm too heavy, and after many efforts I find a current that lands me, a thread of curly singe, on the back of her shirt at the collar. I try to gather my thoughts. This takes several years. I am memory, this I know. I'm also ashy words. High in the sky, heavy, I saw our story crying.

I want no more crying.

Chapter 2
Our Story

Dreamer. Crazy. Liar. Such an imagination inside that little head. Kimberly heard those words when she burned me on the hill. Crazy. Liar. Dreamer. Words from long ago when she was a little kid. She wasn't a little kid when she held the flaming stick. She was fifty. Really old. Still, she heard the words.

When Kimberly was a little kid words on a page looked real. They didn't change like people do. They sat on paper. Stayed the same. She knew that she could trust them. I want her to trust me too. I'm doing this for her. I grip my pencil tight and wait for words to come.

That blank is me waiting. My problem (it's our problem) is how to tell the truth. I once read a story (I can't remember which) where a man held up a pencil and spun a globe till it stopped. Wherever he put the pencil down is where he had to go. I like the idea of this. It might help with truth. I spin myself now in Kimberly's brain to see where the pencil lands. It sends me (after I've spun) to Los Angeles and a desk.

Los Angeles. Second grade. Year eight in Kimberly time.

In year eight (Kimberly time) I write a book report every day. Some days I write a hundred. Miss Fern tells me stop. But but but

"The prize?" (That's Miss Fern.)

I nod my little head.

"You've won it once, that's enough. Give your friends a chance."

She's talking about my classmates, none of whom I know. Do you like the use of "whom?" Captain Grammar tells me "whom." I like rules. (Me or I? Object? Subject? Which?) Miss Fern says I'm quiet. That's when I say thank you.

The book report prize is a golden squirrel with shiny ruby eyes. Miss Fern tells me pin him on but that might tear my blouse. I put him in his box. He clatters when I shake it. The golden squirrel is talking! I run with him from school shaking his box in my hand. I freeze at the Wilshire underpass that's green and has an echo. It scares me when I'm alone but now I have the squirrel. "Fa-la-la I love you squirrel!" I race through the Wilshire underpass and make it to my house. I run upstairs to my room. "Once again we've cheated death." My father likes to say that.

I open the box at my desk. "Come out little squirrel, be happy." I lift him from his cotton pad and no, oh no no. A ruby eye is gone. I ran too fast. I shook his box. I deserve to die. I prick my hand with his pin. I drip my blood in the eye hole. I pick up a pencil. Start.

Title of Book: _Cultures of Sacrifice_

Author: _Mabel May_

Story: _Long ago times like Aztec and Mayan had human sacrifice. They cut out hearts from a body and held them up to a god. The gods aren't here anymore but some of the temples exist. People got painted blue._

Favorite Part: _Painted blue._

Least Favorite Part: _Kids got their hearts cut too._

Draw A Picture From The Book:

My drawing is not as good as a real artist which I would like to be if I had talent. It shows a girl on a temple ledge about to get sacrificed. The ? in her bubble is "Can I keep my heart?" She's ready to sacrifice herself for all people but wants to leap off the ledge with her heart still in her body. That's against the rules.

In book reports there's rules. The book report form Miss Fern hands out has lines that look like _____ . When you write your words on book report _____s the story's already made so you can't get in trouble. You can if you make your own.

In Kimberly's story I'm a new kid at Beverly Vista Elementary. I went to first grade in a different school in Los Angeles. I went to kindergarten in Madison, Wisconsin where you wear snowsuits. You don't wear snowsuits in Los Angeles. That means your knees show. Mine are knobby so they bump into furniture and rock walls but I don't mind. Scabs are interesting things to examine and rub in your fingers. You can also drop them in cereal bowls before giving them to your brother which I never do. My brother Jim is one year younger. My sister Eliza is three years younger. I'm the oldest so I'm in charge.

My father is Captain Grammar. Chaos of word is chaos of thought. A verb acts and a pronoun sits while adjectives jeer or praise. My father is an adjective. My mother is a pronoun. I'd love to be a verb. My favorite thing is a ?. Meaning a question mark. A ? looks like a slide. Or turn it upside down. Then you have a swing.

At school I float mean kids in thought bubbles then walk through halls of water with fish mouths opening wide. Row row row your boat. Do songs get stuck in your head? I say thoughts and songs and pieces of color swirl around in a brain like flavor in an ice cream cone. Not the balls of hard ice cream, the soft kind that's pressed from a machine and spirals with a point. I call them twisted wizard hats. When they melt I watch them change and wonder if a brain does that. In Los Angeles there's

Oh, I hear my name. I have to stop, have to _____.

This _____ is not a book report. This _____ is me tossed high. I flip and twirl and land and I'm very very important. My book gets pulled from the desk. My father lifts the book. I wait for the game we'll play and keep my eyes wide open. No. Oh no no. He's the empty monster no one sees but me. He holds the book in the air then presses it on my face. I breathe in words and paper (blue, Mayan, stone) as I crawl inside my heart. My heart gets small. Smaller. Invisible.

Kimberly shoots from our body. She lands up on the ceiling then turns her face aside. I watch her hover there, the way she always does, and pray that she won't leave. Sometimes she leaves me all alone and no, oh no no, she slips herself through the window and disappears like light. I scream for her

9

return, but it's a no-noise scream. If anyone hears me scream (not that anyone would) it's instant death by drowning.

During my no-noise screams there's words and paper pressing. There's father. There's hair grabbed. There's funny tingles. There's fingers. There's open your legs. There's begging no. There's say you like it. There's begging no. There's shut your mouth. There's start of pain. There's calling it love, calling it love, calling it calling it calling it as I swirl my imagination and press it through solid things. I enter pages. I walk through pictures. I travel into dream as pink life slides like a slithering snake into the world of my dungeon mind where I've made a sacrifice ledge.

I stand up tall on the dungeon mind ledge and scream my no-noise screams. Throngs raise up their fists. You die for us! For the good of all! For all! For all! For all! I hear their cheers and wild cries until I hear my mother. If my mother calls my name I have to set the table. I pull myself from the dungeon mind and walk myself downstairs. Fork near spoon. Forget. Cup near plate. Forget. My mother calls me good girl and sends me back upstairs.

Upstairs I stand in my room. I look out the window onto a parking lot where grass pokes up from cracks. If I were outside I'd lie down on the hot cement and watch ants crawl onto my finger.

Instead I remember tomorrow. Tomorrow I'll ride in the dented grey station wagon which is a chariot my mother flies to special days at the beach. I'll sit in the back seat with Jim and Eliza and we'll stick our heads out the window yelling wheeeeeee into the air. In the ocean I'll float face down, spread out my arms, open my legs, spin like a dying starfish. Who will save me? Who? A gull will grab my swimsuit strap and swoop me to the sky. He'll open his beak and oh no no, I'll fall spinning down, starfish in a cartwheel, till I crash through the ocean and swarms of fish and land on my dungeon mind ledge. They'll open me up with a rock blade tool. They'll lift my heart with their hands. It will still be beating!

I play these games for years. For all of Kimberly's life. I stand up tall in the dungeon mind waiting on the ledge. My chest gets bared in front of throngs and I feel so very Oh. I'm looked at here with reverence, yes, I'm so important, I can stand up proud, ready to give, take me! I've no need for a heart! Until I see a yawn. A bored guy blow his nose. Then I know a truth. Throngs don't care who I am. They're here to watch me die.

Whenever I know this truth I call for Kimberly's help. "Help me Kimberly, save me!" but she can't really come. She doesn't live in the dungeon mind and doesn't know it exists. If I want to be with her (I always do) I have to wait for a reason. Some kind of stress or pull from her that jumps me from the dungeon mind and into the place she likes. A place she calls real life. I don't like real life. I only go there for her.

I haven't felt a pull from her since the day of the birthday burn. I know she wants me gone (having burned the words on the hill) so I try to obey her wishes and leave her the hell alone. That's why I'm stunned, in year fifty-five, to feel a tug of need. My foot begins to tingle and my head goes very light. I slide from the ledge of dungeon mind, liquid in a drain, until I land, shocked and surprised, inside her gray Toyota.

A sparkle shines in her eyes but I can't read the mood. I kick the back of her seat. I'm still unseen unheard, a little spook of air. A truck pulls up in the mirror and it rolls and sways and barrels by, shaking me like a rattle. Kimberly's grip is steady. Her hands look old on the steering wheel, wrinkled skin and veins, so I try a magic spell. "Come back to us, oh years, the years of long ago!" My spell is dumb and useless. It's year fifty-five now (Kimberly time) and her eyes are squinty and bright as they stare at I-70W.

I watch her blowing hair (brown, dyed, the window's down) and feel a surge of love. If she could see me now I'd beg for a chocolate cake. She'd bake me one herself. I'd eat the entire thing. I'd wipe the crumbs with a doily then ask (oh very politely) if I could stay forever. She'd look at me like I'm nuts and say "you gotta go."

I know she has to say it. I stink like a dead sock. All the years in invisible heart left a terrible reek. Kimberly (so unfair) smells like a fist of roses. She shot from our body every time so she was left untouched.

If you've ever shot from your body you know why I can't explain it. The invisible heart is a mystery the brain creates for itself. It's a place of no escape where you think you'll die (you know you'll die) so your body shoots away. The self explodes. It shatters like hit glass. It hurls shards of you into a place you can't see and the shards become their own thing with their own opinions and emotions and annoying habits and crazy attitudes and they crash around in your life like they own it. I know this because I'm a shard. But I'm not bossy or crazy and I'm never annoying at all. I'm probably Kimberly's favorite. The other shards flew off (ashes zooming past) so I'm the last one left.

Which doesn't mean I'm soul. Soul sounds way too braggy. I'm memory. Ashy words. A song in Kimberly's head. Sometimes I sound like a kid. Other times like a genius. I'm lying about the genius. But I do go philosophical when I get really scared.

I'm a bit scared now in the car. Kimberly burned me up because I made a mistake. The rule of invisible heart was hide it. Keep it shut. It held the no-noise screams that no one wants to hear. I followed the rule (I made the rule) until one day I couldn't. In year thirty-seven (Kimberly time) my throat got loud and open. I don't know why, I never will, but I let out a no-noise scream that suddenly had a noise. I screamed and screamed and screamed until Kimberly un-forgot.

The invisible heart ripped open and out came the burst of shards. Little One, brown eyes blank, a shard from year four to eight. Wisp, her hair in braids, a shard from year nine to ten. Lola, wild and sassy, a shard from older years. Me (my name is Red Girl) a shard who looked like a knobby-kneed girl wearing a raggy tunic. A streak of red ran down my leg and trickled toward my foot. When Kimberly saw the streak life-as-we-knew-it changed. I smiled when she saw me but my smile didn't help. Our father Captain Grammar called me crazy liar. Our frightened pronoun mother told me keep it quiet. Eliza and Jim couldn't hear me, wouldn't hear me, no, so Kimberly lost our family because I broke the rule.

She cried and cried and cried. It was very hard. She did her best to love me. She gave us therapy time. Trips to the zoo. Massages. A million baths with bubbles. She rocked me in her arms. Fed me chocolate cake. She tried to love me for thirteen years until she gave up trying. She couldn't love me, ever, no matter what we did, so in year fifty (Kimberly time) she pushed the wheelbarrow up the hill and lit the flaming stick.

I kick her seat again, this time feeling guilt. "I'm sorry I'm sorry I'm sorry I made you un-forget!" She rolls up the open window and her hair stops blowing wild. In the tangle of her hair I see some streaks of gray. It's year fifty-five (she's old and done) so what's the point of sorry. I pull my feet in close. I don't want to kick her seat. I also don't want to die. Kimberly's driving to Santa Fe and she's driving very fast. If she were to see I'm still around she might flip the car.

Chapter 3
Zen and the Invisible Heart

In the car to Santa Fe Kimberly's not alone. Tikko lies in the passenger seat reading a stack of papers. Tikko's not his real name (I've changed it for Kimberly's story) but Tikko himself exists. When he opens his mouth Kimberly acts like pearls are dropping and she often laughs out loud. I never see what's funny. They've been dating two years and I haven't laughed once.

Kimberly lives in Manhattan (the Upper West Side for years) so the long flat rope of I-70W looks empty and strangely open. No buildings looming large, nothing to break the sky. Her mind (I know her mind) is slightly detached as the lines of the road hypnotize with rhythm. She's driving to Santa Fe where she and Tikko will stay for a week. Then he'll fly to New York while she drives herself to Taos.

"Three months alone in Taos. Maybe I'll go crazy." (That's Kimberly.)

She laughs her laugh when she says this (Tikko smiles too) but I wonder now, maybe, if Taos is the reason I'm here. When she applied for the time in Taos she wrote on her application "I need to leave real life." Which meant she needed open space, time to come alive, and she's telling Tikko (eyes on the road) that she hopes the sky of New Mexico will wake her like a gong.

I stare at the back of their heads. It's Kimberly's tangled hair and Tikko's stubbly buzz cut. Tikko is quiet and calm when he's not telling stupid jokes. I like him for that (she does too) but I never know what he's thinking. They met in New York through a mutual friend. The friend and Tikko, years ago, took the same French language class while both of them lived in Paris. Tikko (the friend told Kimberly) was at that time so quiet it seemed he could barely speak. He had just moved to Paris, and he'd moved to Paris from Japan where he'd lived a good long time, maybe a bit too long, in a monastery. Zen. Where you sit in meditation for many many hours and maybe (the friend told Kimberly) lose your power of speech.

Kimberly knew of Tikko when she was still married and younger. She had wondered, at times, hearing her friend, about his unusual life. In year twenty-one (Tikko time) he stopped believing in God. He was a serious Christian, raised this way in Wyoming, and the sudden loss of belief truly almost killed him. He worked a hotel night job on summer break from college and spent his afternoons trying not to open his closet. The closet held his rifle, which he wanted to use on himself, so he kept the closet locked for many many weeks until, at the hotel night job (thankfully he was alone) his brain went into a focus, a kind of concentration, that ended in explosion. All notions of self and thought blew up in a wordless bliss. A radiance revealed. A world of illusion lost. He stumbled home to his room, the sun still low in Wyoming, and spent some days (two? three?) in a state of shock and wonder.

Later, after years, he could name this explosion satori (Zen) or a mystical seeing (Eckhart) but at the time all he knew was something strange had happened. Something he couldn't explain, not with words, there are no words, and it seems to me, because of this, a bit like invisible heart. But beautiful, Tikko says. It changed his life completely. He taught English in Japan (he did this after college) to save enough money to travel the world and meditate very deeply. He rarely feels alone (he knows we're not alone) and hearing him read from his book in the car makes me want satori.

Satori sounds like empty space, at least from what I'm hearing, but I start to imagine a taffy sky where everyone floats around in happy-go-lucky bubbles. The bubbles never pop. They bob along in the taffy sky which I imagine in detail as Tikko reads from his papers.

"I woke on a strange new planet but that is actually backwards. The entire world I'd constructed since childhood -- a world where I was a separate being among other separate beings -- was revealed to have been a self-made dream. What was left? A world without the constructs of the human mind, unmediated by intellect. And what to call this state in which no individual things or selves exist, only the nothingness of All? I circle back to "God" -- as good a word as any -- but naming God is cutting the sea with a knife. If you mean anything at all by the word "God," even the least little thing, then "God" cannot exist, as God is beyond all categories of existence and non-existence."

His book has a working title which is only a working title. It's "An Atheist's Mystical Journey" and what does Kimberly think? I don't hear what she thinks as I'm lost in thoughts of God. I used to see God as a circus ringmaster who held a thin whip. He looked like a cartoon drawing and certainly wasn't cutting the sea with a knife or pulsing beyond existence. These days I see God as a giant sheet of Saran wrap stretched across the sky. I try to imagine a biblical God, or Norse, Hindu, Navajo, but my thoughts go off in a swirl until finally (for this I'm thankful) I come back to Kimberly's voice.

"....and also, well you know this, I get pretty jealous when I hear what you describe. It sounds like bliss or terror, I mean it sounds like both, and I wish I could understand it, like really understand it, but now, and don't laugh yet, I'm seeing this taffy sky, this stretched out pinkish sky, and people in bubbles floating around waving like la-la forever and oh come on, come on, I said don't laugh just yet."

Both of them are laughing, punchy from the car, and I grit my teeth as they laugh their laughs that sound like ridiculous barks. Tikko's laugh is light (he's kind and indulgent with her) but Kimberly's covers a wish to understand what she can't understand no matter how hard she tries. Her face goes suddenly soft. I watch her eyes, dark and brown, squint with a touch of headache. Kimberly has a tension line that sits between her eyes. It throbs whenever she thinks too hard or whenever memory presses. I feel myself in her tension line and have a jolt of oh no.

Captain Grammar (our father) wrote books on religious poetics. The books were academic (Donne, Milton, Herbert) and growing up with his books around put many words in my ears. "God," "Infinite," "Oneness," bob through my head like floaters, and now I sit in a young girl's dress, fighting with words too large (Buber's I and Thou, Kierkegaard's Christian Discourses) on the bouncing knee of my father. The words rise up like monsters with powerful pointy teeth. They eat my young girl thoughts and spit them out like candy. They drag me over a knee. They toss me onto a sofa.

They yell and proclaim and whisper and snipe that what I think is real's not real and what's not real is fact. That's what happens with no-noise screams and years of invisible heart. You live in real/not real and flit between the two. I rant on myself, angry now, as I see what a mess I've made. Instead of blissful taffy sky Kimberly's in a flashback.

Flashbacks start with a headache. Kimberly feels a throbbing that builds and builds and builds until she wants to throw up. I hide in flashbacks (I cause them) as I rumble around in her cells, a hum of background noise, unless she wants to see me. Which after the burning is never, so I curl up now on my father's knee deep inside Kimberly's forehead.

"My head is starting to pound, I think I need a break." (Kimberly.)

Tikko reaches for a bottle of water. He believes water can cure headaches so he hands it to Kimberly. She holds it against her forehead, hoping for some coolness, but the bottle has gone lukewarm. She unscrews the cap with her teeth and takes a tiny sip.

"Sorry. I left for a while. My dad popped into my head."

"Oh that guy."

"Yeah, it sucks. Sorry again. The water helps. Give me a minute, okay?"

Kimberly rubs her forehead, pressing it with her thumb, while clenching her stomach tight inside and taking fifteen breaths. Then she smiles at Tikko.

"I'm back." (Kimberly.)

"Are you sure?"

"Yeah oh yeah I'm good. So listen, here's a question. How does one drop the past? And can it really be dropped? Wait, that's not the question. What I mean is this. Is self a describable thing? Because, and this is me, I think we all have many selves, many many parts, that can, at least for me, create this inner chaos that comes up when I'm still. I mean if I try to meditate. Normal?"

"It can be normal. It's different for every person."

"And when I try to meditate I see this little ghost kid curled up in a jail. She wears a raggy tunic and has some blood on her leg. This happens after I sit for a while, asking "who am I?" on breaths. It bothers me when I see her, and I try to let her go, but when I manage that I feel this aching lonely thing that kind of takes me over. Normal?"

"Well, what's normal?"

Kimberly laughs a little laugh then touches her tongue to her lip. Tikko speaks again.

"I think that going quiet, being alone with breath, reveals the self to itself. All kinds of crap

23

comes up. Monsters, fears, visions. You see them. Get to know them. Then push them away as Maya."

"Maya?"

"Means illusion."

Kimberly passes a truck. The driver lifts his hand, fingers long and shaky, and waves to us from his window. Kimberly doesn't see him. She's opened a pack of gum, Trident cinnamon flavor, and put a piece in her mouth. The smell of cinnamon fills the car as Kimberly chews and talks.

"The lonely thing is awful. I mean it's really awful. Though I've had a few moments of something, not like what you're talking about, a total oneness thing, but tiny little moments, usually in nature, where I feel a kind of expanse that ripples out, calm, like rings on a body of water. I had it once on a lake."

She takes a sip of water then screws the lid back on. I know she's trying to decide if she wants to continue or not. Kimberly's open with Tikko, but what she's about to say she's never said to anyone and it feels, I feel it with her, like giving up a secret.

"I call it elusive love. I mean, because it's elusive. It's like this huge enormous love, this blissful state of being, that lasts for only a minute and then it disappears. I wish I could bottle it up, you know? Have it on tap whenever."

A silence sits in the car while I think of elusive love. I felt it with her, on the lake, years and years ago. It was before she un-forgot, she didn't know I existed, but the two of us had joined, dissolved somehow as one, and I was her, and she was me, and we weren't in our secret war, our endless secret war, of who is who and what is real. The ripples of lake expanded, the ripples were clear and pure. It was a tiny moment. Brief and yet forever. I want it back, so does she, at least I think she does, but now I hear her sighing, talking about the past, how to drop it, how, she really wants it gone. Tikko mentions koans, Zen riddles such as "who am I?" which are designed to force you through thought walls that block your no-self nature. It's thought that constructs illusion. Thought constructs a past. Thought is self. Thought is memory. Thought can be released.

"So where does memory go?" (Kimberly.)

She's read of an experiment with laboratory rats who pass fear-memory on to their babies. The rats get shocked by electricity when they smell a certain smell. When their babies and grandbabies are born they're afraid of the same smell even though they're never shocked.

I wonder now if I'm an epigenetically inherited fear that comes from a thousand years of ? in my biological heritage. I wonder if I'm a faulty neurotransmitter in Kimberly's brain or a residual depression or a clang of anxiety trapped in her nervous system. I know I'm the stink of dead sock. What I don't know is why I torture Kimberly. I stick around, never leave, I blow through her life like a blinding need that I'm not proud of, no no no, but maybe I can maybe I can maybe I can

Stop. Slow down. Think.

Title of Book: _Memory Thoughts_

Author: _Me_

What Is Memory: _A shape shifter_

How Does Memory Behave: _It tries hard. It consolidates. It chooses what to see. It creates story from itself. It hurls trauma rocks at Kimberly. It makes flashbacks. It seeps into cells._

Where Does Memory Live: _It's homeless. To seek shelter it wanders from secret dungeon minds to the outside world to time eternal._

Does Memory Have Free Will: _I hope so._

Tikko picks up his pages. I see them shake in his hand as I listen to him read. "The spiritual world _is_ the material world and the material world _is_ the spiritual world." I press my hands together and wonder if I'm the world. I know I'm solid to myself (my hands press hard together) but invisible as the air. "Enlightenment is the trick of killing the self and yet retaining consciousness. Buddhist sages liken the effort required to that of a mosquito attacking an iron bowl."

Mosquito! I'll be a mosquito. I'll attack the iron bowl of Kimberly who's driving fifteen miles over the speed limit.

She slaps her hand on the steering wheel and spits her gum out the window. I'm surprised by this. I've known of her distress (I've made my contributions) but now I see its depth. She unwraps a fresh piece of Trident with her teeth. She chews it like a praying mantis while telling Tikko she can't wait to get to the exit for Joplin, Missouri. What she means is get out of the car. It's become oppressive, and Kimberly's easily trapped.

In Joplin, Missouri Kimberly and Tikko want to check out the Bonnie and Clyde house. When they step out of the car they're blasted by heat that's melted tar patches. They stumble a few blocks under the drip of trees left standing from a hurricane and search the horizon. The Bonnie and Clyde house is highlighted on the highway brochure but the map doesn't match what they see. They wander around and consider. They comment on desolation. They wonder if the house exists, and if it does, is it worth finding? Kimberly shrugs her shoulders, sweat streaking her neck.

"What do you want to do?" (Kimberly.)

"Get back into the car."

Driving west from Joplin they watch the country sag. Sometimes they point or note. "There. A sign of hardship." Tikko puts the brochure in the glove compartment.

"What money buys is time. Time's the most valuable thing." (Tikko.)

Kimberly turns a dial. Cold air blasts through the car as they talk about money and time. Tikko has little money but Kimberly has enough. She didn't always, not at all, so she knows what it can buy. Transformation. Safety. Fear of multiple choice. Her husband came from money and he shared it with her freely. They were together twenty years and she's lucky as hell, she knows this (though divorce is far from fun) but she did, and this is a problem, notice, having money, that she often felt quite useless. Worthless, even. Pointless. She'd never had time to think before (always trying to survive) so the freedom money brought hit her like a rock. All the loathing of self, the tentacles of slime, the wagging nasty fingers that slithered up like snakes and pointed at her, mean, accusing her of dirt, being dirt, worthless, a grubby crumpled sock, a little piece of spit, swirled up from her insides and she wonders now, with Tikko, if her forgotten memories would have come without money. She had the time to think back then, well, she still has time, but thoughts, oh god, the thoughts, how do you shut them up?

"Well, you can't." (Tikko) "You have to

"Yeah, I know. Turn them into Maya. Get rid of the little fucks."

I can't believe my ears. Maya? Little fucks? Is that what she thinks of me? I hurl myself back to the dungeon mind (jumping there from the car) and scream in thwarted love. I want to be understood! I want to be hugged and seen! Show me a person who hasn't been hurt or made a secret world!

Kimberly laughs from the car and I want to pull her face off. I saved her life with invisible heart. Without that place of shooting away she might have gone crazy. Might have died. I let her shoot to the ceiling. I let her leave me with him. I lived through it all, all of it, all, so she could stay untouched. I climb to the sacrifice ledge to yell at throngs below.

"The mind can shatter open! The mind can re-create! The mind can dream itself!"

I hear the echo of me and sit myself on the ledge. I swing my feet, calming down, trying not to go all dramatic. I've been accused of that, many times, too many, by Kimberly and others. Dreamer. Crazy. Liar. Such an imagination inside that little head.

I look around the dungeon mind then bloom in sudden pride. Yes, imagination. Yes, my little head. Here I'm safe with truth. A father can hurt his kid. A dungeon mind can protect. I wrap myself in its softness, a gauzy thrill of love, and curl myself up on the sacrifice ledge feeling so very Oh. I gaze at the stones of dungeon mind (they sometimes change their colors) and rest inside this wonderful world I made all by myself.

Chapter 4
Dungeon Mind

The dungeon mind belongs to me. Kimberly's never seen it. Though what she calls her life, her so important real real life, can sometimes cause a change in here I hardly ever like.

When I first made the dungeon mind it was me on the ledge alone (cheering throngs don't count) until Kimberly un-forgot. That's when all the shards, Little One, Lola, Wisp and me, burst from invisible heart. After the burst from invisible heart Kimberly saw us in real life (her so important real real life) but we mostly hid in the dungeon mind deep inside her being. We lived here together, happy, fighting sometimes but making up, as if we were a family, or some idea of family, until Kimberly walked up the hill, wheelbarrow banging full, and Little One, Lola and Wisp flew away as ash.

I uncurl myself now on the ledge. Kimberly hurt me with her words (Maya? Little fucks?) and I'm tired of our fighting. It doesn't look like fighting (no one can see inside) but there's a war going on with us for who gets to be in charge. War might be dramatic. Maybe the word is skirmish. We're in a constant skirmish that keeps us both entangled, trapped together, knotted, and it's not good for either. In fact it's quite exhausting. All the headaches, flashbacks, random days of stupor, who wants to live like that?

I walk down the steps of the ledge to distract myself from her. The dungeon mind is gorgeous. It shimmers with magical light that refracts from the lava stones. The lava stones are anger that comes from Kimberly's life but I polish them up in dungeon mind and make them look like pearls. They're purple, green, red, whatever color Kimberly wants (or whatever I think she wants) and I polish them up with my little head that's stuffed with imagination. Yes, imagination. Yes, my little head. But I'm no crazy liar. Let's get that straight right now. Everything I imagine here is true in Kimberly's life.

I follow the path of lava stones that leads to Wisp's old tree. Wisp (though I shouldn't say this) is my very favorite shard. She's from year nine to ten (Kimberly time of course) and lived in Indiana. Kimberly's family moved a lot in her so important real real life. Born in Pennsylvania. Jim born in Nebraska. Eliza born in Wisconsin. Then Los Angeles, France, Indiana (that's where Colin's born) and the little state of Delaware. Our parents liked to move and our father often had to. Master's degree Nebraska. PhD Wisconsin. Then college teaching and on and on but Wisp was in Indiana and yes, my favorite shard.

Here's why I like Wisp. She climbed trees. She read books. She told all jerks to stuff it. I stand now under her tree and look up into the branches. She used to read up there, sitting on a branch, pretending she couldn't be found. If she wasn't reading in a tree she was racing and running around or getting lost on purpose. She often held my hand when I really needed to cry. All she had to do was touch my hand and hold it and I'd get a sense of a-okay and fa-la-la and yes.

Little One couldn't do that. When she and I held hands I wanted to pull her inside me to save her save her save her. She was year four to eight and very very shy. Her eyes were often dark and blank and she liked to hide in closets. I peek inside her closet now to see what she left behind. Our mother's ballet toe shoes. Our father's unlaced Oxfords. The ribbons of the toe shoes are tied up like a swing and the tongue in one of the Oxfords has been cut with a pair of scissors. Little One wasn't always shy. She had a sense of humor if you could get her going.

Lola could get her going. She was a shard from older years and lived in Delaware. Lola could give two shits (she said this fairly often) about what the rest of us thought. She swayed her hips and smoked her smokes and drank her gin and tonics. She knew the effect she had. She was fierce and immortal and all of us wanted to feel the respect she handed out like never. She dumped the butts of cigarettes and left her gin and tonics on every surface she touched. I pick up one of her ice cubes now (a miracle it's still frozen) and smell a scent of gin.

The gin cracks me. I suddenly start to wail and miss them all like a long-lost limb. I push my fists in my eyes. Fists can stop the tears (stupid stupid tears) but not the crush of lonely ache I feel inside my chest.

I stumble myself (with drama) toward the only person here. She's not really a person, not like me and the shards, but she has a face at least. Except it never moves. Nothing about her moves. All she does is stare while gripping her wooden pencil. On her desk is the golden squirrel (the second-grade book report prize) who's missing a ruby eye. I don't know what she is, or why she's frozen solid, but she's been here since un-forgetting. I wouldn't be near her at all now if I weren't hurt and lonely. Again, Kimberly's doing. She pulled me into her car, her stupid gray Toyota, and made me go all hopeful before she got insulting. This is our inner war, excuse me, inner skirmish. I get lulled, pulled to her, thinking this time, maybe, she'll look at me with love, listen to sorry sorry, but then she shows her colors (putrid green and phlegm) and I start to hate her guts. We split in two in invisible heart and if I knew how to fix that I'd call myself a genius, I'd call myself a god, I'd call myself a super girl who

Stop. Slow down. Calm.

Title of Book: _Who's in Charge._

Author: _Whoever wins._

Story: _Un-forgotten memory seeks love and union. Real life fights her hard_.

Favorite Part: _Elusive love._

Least Favorite Part: _Lonely._

Draw A Picture From The book:

((((((((( )))))))))) ← ripples on the lake.

I put my report on the desk. The girl-at-her-desk can't see it (I'm making that assumption) but at least my eyes are dry. No more tears. No more tears. I'll call for the Laughing Corpse.

I made the Laughing Corpse. He loves me no matter what I do, even if it's stupid. After Kimberly un-forgot it was a time of chaos, horrible pain, horrible loss, and I needed some compassion so I found a stash of bones. I picked them up. Hefted each. Strung them all together and put a skull on top. The skull burst into a cackling laugh that made me wildly happy. The Laughing Corpse is my rock. He keeps me strong. Invincible. Safe. We're together always, well most of the time at least, so now, as I look around, I start to get real nervous. Kimberly could have zapped him. Blown him up. Sent him off. I wouldn't put that past her, not after "little fucks."

I shout his name as I run the paths, wading through piles of paper, torn from books, books she's read, words she loved in her real real life but now are words she's forgotten, piling up, piling high, higher and higher every year like leaves unraked in fall. I dive in a pile of paper. I huddle under the crush. I press my hands together and hope my calls are heard. Please. Please. Please. Let him be alive.

I hear his cackling laugh. He tells me a corny joke ("Knock knock, who's there, boo-hoo why are you crying?") as he pulls me out of the papers. He brushes a page from my head and I hug his bones in joy.

"I thought you were dead!" (Me.)

He takes off his hat (a flat beret) and spins it on his finger. His hat becomes the invisible heart (you can see it for just a moment) till he spins it back to a hat then flips it onto his skull. To cheer me up for sure he pulls out his ukulele and sings my favorite song. "Nobody likes me, everybody hates me, guess I'll go eat worms." I sing along to the words, dancing as I do, till he lifts the ukulele and waves it in a triumph.

"I'm the Laughing Corpse! I will never die!"

I laugh (he's so dramatic, more than I'll ever be) but then I go all serious.

"Okay, whatever, except

I don't know how to continue. I sit myself down on his skeleton knees and let out a big huge sigh. Then I wiggle my toes, twirl my hair with a finger, until he finally asks.

"What is it Red Girl?"

"I don't know."

"Kimberly?"

"How did you guess?"

"It's always Kimberly, isn't it?"

I tell him the story as best I can. My getting pulled to the car, Kimberly going to Taos, my giving her a flashback, my sorry sorry sorry. The Laughing Corpse raises his hand.

"Stop. I know what you're doing. You're blaming yourself for invisible heart."

"Because

"No, stop."

He takes off his hat and spins it. We see the invisible heart, just for a tiny moment, but he doesn't stop the spinning.

"There's a reason I keep this for you."

"I know I know I know

"The invisible heart is not your fault. Threats of a knife to your neck. Pillows on your face. Laughed at when you told. You had to split from Kimberly, there was no other choice."

"Yeah, but now

37

"No. She's never going to love you. Stay with me in the dungeon mind and forget about her, forget it."

"But I'm still getting pulled. My feet are tingling now, my head feels strange and light, she needs me for something."

"Right. She needs you to kick around."

"That's not true."

"For what then?"

"She needs me for --- I don't know! I want to fly as ash! Little One, Wisp and Lola did! What's wrong with me? What's wrong?"

The Laughing Corpse grips my shoulder.

"There's nothing wrong with you."

I jump up from his knees, startled by my outburst. The Laughing Corpse puts his hat back on and speaks with an urgent voice.

"They flew because they're lightweights. You're no lightweight, Red Girl. You're the greatest ever. A sacrifice girl extraordinaire who can die for the good of all without even blinking an eye. Kimberly doesn't deserve you. No one alive deserves you."

My feet start tingling hard and my head's a pink balloon.

"I'm getting pulled to Kimberly."

"Take this for protection."

He breaks off one of his fingers (they grow like lizard tails) and presses it in my hand.

"Don't let this one go. Love will keep you safe." (Laughing Corpse.)

I swirl like liquid, clutching the bone, till I hear the car radio crackle. Tikko's turned it on. Static first, then country. I tie the bone in my hair as I fall asleep to twangs of love, love you till you die, you ain't worth the whiskey and the good lord high above is singing the same ole song.

Chapter 5
A Hollow Thing

When I open my eyes we're in Santa Fe. Kimberly looks excited as she pulls the bags from the car. At the guesthouse desk, getting the key, she hears about Zozobra. Tonight, this very night, is the evening he'll be burned.

Zozobra was made as a joke in 1924. He was only two feet tall. Now he's a fifty-foot puppet, dressed in a big tuxedo, who's been burned every year in Fiesta Week since 1926.

"Do you want to go?" (Kimberly to Tikko.)

"Yeah but I feel like shit."

Tikko had an appendectomy last week. That's why he lay in the passenger seat while Kimberly did the driving. Now he sits by the fireplace kiva that bulges into the living room like a round urn. Kimberly lifts her suitcase and carries it into the bedroom. She showers in the stone tiled bathroom. She lets the water wash off four days of driving and all of Manhattan while she yells through the door to Tikko.

"I think I want to see it!" (Kimberly through the door.)

There's a crowd on the curved dirt road. Many men wear hats (cowboy, baseball, brimmed) while women swish their hair. Kimberly's tall and pale in the crowd and gulps thin air like a fish. Her blood's still at the level of sea so her heart beats quick and light. I dance and skip and pull her along, come on come on let's go.

At the entrance to the park she waits in a winding line while bags are inspected for guns. She opens her bag, walks past the rope, then wanders through blankets and chairs. There's a singer who sings in Spanish as electric guitars blare loud. Kimberly sways to the sound as she looks out onto the field. Coolers. Kids with chicken. Some of them run with pinwheels. There's a special train tonight to Albuquerque. A man behind her laughs. "Don't listen to that announcement. That train never comes."

The sky darkens and the mayor of Santa Fe appears. She speaks into a microphone with a voice half-solemn half-joke. "Now we let Zozobra take our glooms. Some have been sent from far away. Some are here from you. All tonight will burn."

Glooms that are written on paper get shoved in Zozobra's body. I imagine Kimberly's glooms ("Change" "Aging" "Red Girl") while dancing girls in thin white gowns flutter like baby swans. After they flutter away, Zozobra groans in howling lament as his body bursts into flame. The crowd chants "burn him burn him burn him!" while drums pound, or maybe not, that might not be true, but the pulse of the crowd and the groaning howls create a beat and rhythm that in a war or hanging would feel like rising hate.

Glooms and ash and tuxedo bits fly up into the sky. Some of them go high, mixing in with stars. Others spin to the grass. I start to feel unsteady as I travel back in time. Five years back. Birthday. Kimberly on the hill.

She had called her ex-husband first. Could she use the house upstate? Yes, of course, of course (divorce still new but friendly) so Kimberly loaded the boxes, cardboard and labelled "Someday," then drove four hours north.

The boxes are proof I exist. I don't want them burned. I try to tell Kimberly this, but in the locker room of her gym, many months before, she had heard two women wrapped in towels speak in earnest tones. To convince the body to fully release (one of the towel women said) ritual is important. Burn a thing. Throw it away. Toss it off a bridge. But don't look back. Ever.

When Kimberly sits on the upstate floor cutting the "Someday" boxes, she tells herself that she won't look, won't even read a word, but while she's sitting on the floor, notebooks and papers strewn, her eyes glance over pages.

Letters from our mother ("It's your problem," "I was afraid," "No one believes a wife") written in careful cursive. Letters from our father ("I think you're very sick") typed on unlined paper. Spiral notebooks of dreams, Kimberly's dreams and nightmares, most of them caused by me. She's kept all this in boxes for reasons she can't explain, not that she ever tries, except when the boxes frown, quiet from the closet, accusing her of neglect. Paralysis. Inertia. Waiting for a "Someday." When she'll do what? Show them? Better to get the wheelbarrow. Push it up the hill.

Before she burns the papers I hug the Laughing Corpse. So do Little One, Lola and Wisp. The Laughing Corpse breaks his fingers and gives them to us to hold. Be brave. Be strong. Be wise. Then we're torn away.

Kimberly's fire sends us high. She watches us float in the air as I hang like a fool alone. I see her on the rock. Beyond the rock, way beyond, I see my dungeon mind. The Laughing Corpse looks up, eye sockets open in love, bones stretching for help, begging to not be left. I hold out one of his bones, hoping he can grab it, hoping to pull him with me, but I can't reach him, I can't reach. Little One, Wisp and Lola zoom above my head. The lava stones start melting. Forgotten words start blowing. My whole imagination crushes like a can. I make a decision. Find the wind. I ride it down adrift, knowing I can't leave, knowing I'm still needed, as Zozobra crashes now, falling into a heap, sparks shooting out of his head.

In Santa Fe, in the field, Kimberly's strangely bothered. Zozobra is a puppet, made of wire and paper, but she notices now, hearing the crowd, that she'd hoped against all hope he wouldn't really burn. She laughs and shakes her head. He's hollow inside, empty, so why is she feeling bothered? The park lights flicker on. In sudden harsh fluorescence people pack their coolers, swing their kids on shoulders, wander out to get drunk.

On the dark streets back to the guesthouse Kimberly gets lost. She taps her iPhone map as a group of guys walk by, laughing and joking together. One of them slaps her wrist. "Fuck your fucking smart phone." She walks a little faster. She finds the curved dirt road. The metal door to the guesthouse yard creaks when she pushes it open.

Tikko's sound asleep. He rarely sleeps (insomnia) so this is a surprise. Kimberly wants to talk, tell him about Zozobra, but instead she stands at the bathroom mirror framed with smiling suns. Her eyes are bloodshot red. Her mouth's a collapsed O that drools smoke. She brushes her teeth. She spits. Paper glooms float from her hair. Oh she's tired, tired.

She staggers into bed where I give her a million dreams. One is thick dark smoke, the wheelbarrow bumping empty. She pushes the wheelbarrow down the hill, thick smoke flying behind, then sees our parents young. Behind our parents, holding a stick, I dance in front of a fire. Words and char fall down as I write with my stick in the dirt. I write with loopy letters, large so she can see them, "I'm your favorite gloom."

Chapter 6
Empty Touch

"Did you have a bad dream?" (Tikko.) "I heard you in your sleep."

"Oh god, was I yelling?"

"Only in one of my ears."

Kimberly gets more coffee (she's not a morning person) and sits in front of the kiva.

"I dreamed about my parents. I haven't done that for years. There was all this fire and smoke and oh, I guess from Zozobra."

"How was that?"

"Fun. Kooky. So listen to this dream. My dad was in a jet. My mom was in a cake. The jet makes a kind of sense. My dad did Princeton on ROTC and flew in jets for a while. A bombardier he flew with said "Once again we cheated death" every time they landed. "Once again we cheated death" was like this joke in our house. We'd say it after a car trip or any stupid thing."

I'm not sure Tikko's listening, but Kimberly doesn't stop.

"The Air Force is how he met my mom. He was stationed in Lincoln, Nebraska, and she grew up in Nebraska. This really tiny town, really really tiny, but she went to college in Lincoln where she majored in dance and then, well in those days you just got married. At least according to her. They had me right away. She gave me two reasons for that. One is she wanted a family. The other is birth control fail. I'll never know which is true. The cake is from a photo I saw when I was little. My mom is jumping out, her arms up over her head, and she looks totally gorgeous. I wonder why—I'm sorry. I sound really wound up. Altitude maybe."

"Maybe."

She's not wound up from altitude. It's the press of me. I touched her in the night. She may not remember this (she doesn't mention my presence) but after I wrote with my stick in the dirt I hugged her for a moment. She smelled like trees and smoke and didn't push me away. We stood together, hugging, so she knows I'm with her, I think. At least in dreams at night.

The New Mexico sky is open, it's waking us like a gong, and she wants to say this to Tikko now but she gulps her coffee instead. Tikko goes to the sink. Under the smiling sun mirror there's a pottery bowl of soaps. The soaps are small and round and wrapped with little ribbons. He tosses one in the air and catches it in his hand.

"Plaza now?" (Tikko.)

They walk on the curved dirt road. The plaza is full of stalls and people milling around. Kimberly buys some roasted corn, dusted chile red. She gives a cob to Tikko. He needs to rest for a bit (appendectomy pain) so she walks the plaza alone.

I see a young man in the grass. He's bent in front of an older man whose eyes are shining bright. The older man presses a palm on top of the younger man's head. There's an intake of breath. A jolt of their heads. The touched man looks alert, more alert than before, and I see a joining between them, a kind of elusive love. Kimberly stands near a bulletin board covered in advertisements. Crystals. Shamans. Guides. Journeys of inner vision. The young man rises and walks away, looking changed forever. That's dramatic. No. He looks changed for a moment.

Kimberly tosses her corn cob, then goes searching for Tikko. She finds him leaning against a stage where Hopi kids wait to dance.

"I think I saw a healing." (Kimberly.)

Tikko nods his head, watching the Hopi kids move. Their steps look slow and careful behind the adults in masks. There's a drum and jangling sound that picks up speed, pounding, then stops in a gasp of breath. Tikko and Kimberly clap.

They look at each other. Quiet.

In the dream last night, when I hugged her, Kimberly said she was hollow. I ask her now, trying to be heard, if she thinks I'm hollow too. And if we're doomed (dramatic, I know) by the fact that we're split in two. She doesn't seem to hear me. She talks about power in history (the crushing of the Hopi) as she and Tikko walk. Tikko's very thoughtful, and very very smart, but he holds a distance around him (my impression at least) that I see now in his quiet. Back at the guesthouse, later that night, they drink gin outside.

"I'd like to live on a mountain, way up high with a view." (Tikko.)

"I think you're an eagle type person. Me, I think I'm a groundhog."

Tikko looks at Kimberly. Then he pours more gin. They watch a red streaked sky until the sun drops down. That night, during sex, I pull her from his arm. I'm a small girl calling it love calling it calling it. She's Kimberly touching love without me. I name it empty touch. I call it tap on glass. I watch her turn away as Tikko asks what's wrong.

In the morning they drive to hike. The sky is thin and clear. The sun a perfect coin. They climb steep paths to peer into holes. Petroglyphs. Smoky walls. Occasional graffiti. I think of fish and salt and oceans carving rock. Kimberly thinks of tribes long gone and footsteps lost to war. They stop at the edge of a cliff.

"You see all of time out here." (Kimberly.)

I pick up a pointy rock. An arrowhead? I hold it. Kimberly takes a breath before she speaks again.

"I'm sorry about last night. I'm not sure why I

"It's okay."

"No, it's not okay. That night I went to Zozobra I got this wave of oh no, shit. I feel empty inside. Like nothing's there. Nothing's left. And I woke up this morning with well, yes, the stuff we said in New York, the stuff we said last night. I need to be alone. I don't know why, but I know I do, and I'm sorry, I wish I were

"Yeah, alright, so let's

I don't want to hear it. I flip the rock in my hand and tune out what they're saying. It's yakety yak not ready, yakety yak okay, yakety yak her damage, yakety yak fucked up, yakety yak that Red Girl, yakety yak a problem, yakety yak till I catch my rock, press it into my fist, and jab her hard inside. She doubles over gasping, holding onto her stomach.

"Are you okay?" (Tikko.)

"I think it's the chile from breakfast."

Kimberly knows it's not. She has to know, she has to, but there she goes, there she goes, walking away with Tikko. He doesn't look too troubled (he might even be relieved) but I'm getting mad, really mad, that she blamed me in yakety yak. They're talking now, being friends, as I rant inside my anger.

They go to dinner, hike some more. Dinner, hike, dinner, hike, yakety yakety yak as if I'm not even there. Finally, on Tikko's last night, the two of them sit outside.

Stars poke through the sky, pinpricks in a sail, as Kimberly speaks (again!) of solitude and need. She doesn't say my name this time but I've had an effect, I think. I see her hand away from his, tapping the stem of her glass. Tikko says goodnight. The door clicks shut behind him. Kimberly pours the gin from his glass. Then she drinks alone. I want to ask her a question (am I why you're alone?) but her eyes are distant moons. I jump myself to the dungeon mind to ask the Laughing Corpse.

I land in a pile of pages. He rustles through the papers and holds out his ukulele.

"Grab the neck!" (Laughing Corpse.)

I climb the ukulele until I reach his knee. I sit on his knee in silence till he lifts up both of his feet. Lava goo strings like gum. He rubs the lava in his palms, drying it into stones, then juggles the stones for me.

"This is brand new anger. Hers or yours?" (Laughing Corpse.)

"Mine."

"What got you so angry?"

"She blamed me for their break up."

He stands up and throws the stones.

"That's so unjust! So unfair! You're not in control of her. She could blame fresh divorce. She could blame Tikko's hair. She could blame fear of commitment, fear of boredom, fear of death, whatever those humans fear. All of them are nuts. They do whatever they do and find the reasons later."

He tosses me up in the air and spins me like a top. I laugh when he puts me down.

"Where's your bone of protection?" (Laughing Corpse.)

I lift up my hair where I tied it.

"So remember she can't hurt you. And don't let her push you around."

He strums the ukulele. My feet begin to tingle, my head goes very light, as I swirl back into the night where Kimberly drinks alone.

In the morning she and Tikko drive to the airport. Tikko walks through the gate and both of them smile and wave. Back at the guesthouse sun mirror Kimberly takes three soaps. She holds one to her nose, a scent of desert sage, then puts the soaps in a ziplock bag to pack for her time in Taos. On top of her suitcase tucked in the strap is a piece of notebook paper. She opens the folded note. Tikko's writing is bold.

"Solitude is right. Watch for bears in the mountains."

Tikko loves his bears. Because he grew up in Wyoming he knows what to do when a grizzly's near and how a black bear's different. Kimberly reads the note while sitting on her suitcase.

We all are stumbling pilgrims blind to the glory that is. Prisons are what we make. We peer from within and fear the without and each is brilliant illusion. Kimberly knows this truth but not the way to live it. She'd like to see her prison bars so she can scrape away (fingernails like files) toward patient full escape. Tikko has spoken of darkness, the hacking of stubborn branches, the endless peeling away, of layer after layer until the bolt of something, wordless can't be spoken. Truth does not use words, it flings them off like acorns flying from a tree.

Kimberly folds the note and puts it in her pocket. In her pocket she finds the pointy rock I held for her on the cliff. She rubs her fingers on the point then presses it into her palm.

Chapter 7
El Nino

Yellow crime tape circles the cemetery as we drive out of Santa Fe. Later that week Kimberly checks the news. Yes, they found a body.

On the High Road Kimberly gasps. She feels her heart break seeing things more beautiful than she can stand. This is a landscape of power. Flagrant colors. Uncaring cliffs. Skies like painted plates. It makes her feel like nothing. A twig on the side of the road. Enormous as well. Enormous. As if she were stretched out thin.

She stops at Chimayo. According to the brochure there's two churches, El Santuario and El Nino. In El Santuario she studies painted faces. Open eyes. Open mouths. Looks of grateful shock. There's a hole in the floor of a low stone room that holds a pile of dirt. You scoop up dirt (it's holy) and put it in a bag. She picks up some dirt with her fingers and rubs it into her arm. We wait for an effect (I do, at least, I wait) but nothing seems to happen. She spits on her fingers then wipes them clean on the pocket of her jeans. Crutches hang in another room, lining the wall like coats. Thousands of prayers have been spoken here, miracles have occurred, for some, at least, who've written so, in letters of grateful thanks.

El Nino is for kids. I'm happy to see this beautiful church that was made, the placard says, to please the eyes of children. Inside are wooden birds painted with popping color. The birds are carved so smooth you want to live on their backs. I sweep my gaze on a wing and wish, for a wild moment, the Laughing Corpse could be here. He would love the birds. He would love the colors. The colors are those of the lava stones that gleam in the dungeon mind. The dungeon mind is my church, I decide, as light pours over the birds.

Kimberly touches a beak. I imagine her holding a seed, or maybe a crumb of muffin, and feeding the wooden bird. She stands for a moment, feeding, then walks through a little passage that leads to another room. The room is covered with photos. Faces of kids who smile big and wear a suit or dress. On a ledge there's a pile of tiny shoes, plastic dolls, toys. I look at the sprawling things and want to have them all.

To me a church is pews. Dark wood. Hard. The church in Indiana (a Methodist one on campus) is me and Eliza quiet, sitting in homemade dresses. Jim in uncomfortable pants, our mother touching his shoulder, murmuring into his ear. Our father a patient daddy. Slipping me a crayon. He's never the empty monster here, not in pews with people. The people in pews look crisp. I draw their heads in crayon until they rise (we rise up too) for the glorious times of reading hymns and people singing together, together now, together, all of us out of tune.

When we sit back down in the pews I listen to the man. I strain to understand him, all this talk of God. I decide that heaven (if it exists) is a place where questions get answered. Only the ones you ask on earth and only while you're alive. In the pew I don't ask questions. I hear the sound of his words. Father father father, hallowed be thy name, thy will be done, thy will be done, thy will be done done done. Will pulls me into dream, please no will, please no will, please no will be done. My head drops down, loose at the neck, and I sink into dungeon mind. Kimberly stays in the pew. She's watching a play, a show, a story being spun. She tries to believe (she can't) that she's a part of the story. Loved by God. Tended. A lamb inside a flock. But there's no flock in her story. The flock is beyond the fence. She's in a field alone. The shepherd comes with shears.

Kimberly looks at our mother, murmuring still to Jim. Our father watches the man. She tries to give him the crayon but he pushes her hand away. She buries her face in Eliza's hair. Eliza, little sister,

Eliza, little sister. Eliza giggles and squirms. You're tickling me, don't stop. Eliza, little sister, Eliza, little sister. Kimberly tickles and whispers until, in front of a photo, back in El Nino now, she bursts into sudden sobs.

She cries like a heaving seal. A man walks into the room.

"Children are so important." (The man.)

Kimberly wipes her snot, tries to smile and nod. He looks at her unblinking, suggests she light a votive. She will. (Do you have to be Catholic?) She doesn't light a votive. She stumbles to the car. She puts her head on the steering wheel and stares like a frozen robot. Where's she going. Why. What's a steering wheel. The crying fit has left her dry, empty of her sense.

I untie the bone from my hair. Up and down, up and down, I rub it on her back. Love. Safety. Love. Kimberly lifts her head. She squeezes hard on the steering wheel to find the present moment. She grounds herself as she's been taught, ground, ground, ground, until the moment comes. The moment's beautiful. Gold grass. Parking lot. Sound of a crow somewhere.

She pulls out from the parking lot then drives in a rare deep calm. There's no radio playing but her fingers tap a beat. We rise up over a hill and the world bursts open again. Skies are painted plates.

Cliffs lounge free in the distance. Kimberly laughs out loud as she lifts her hands from the steering wheel, a gesture of amazement, then puts them down in awe. She holds this joy the entire drive, all the way to Taos.

Chapter 8
Adobe Promise

At the Taos visitor center there's a woman with a pierced tongue. She doesn't know where the residency is. "Is that where you're going honey?" Kimberly drives around lilting "Is that where you're going honey?" at each turn. She stops at the Walmart of Taos. Inside the Walmart there's a boy with a curve of sculpted hair looped on top of his head and a guy with tattoos all over his face. Kimberly buys a Snickers bar and eats it in the car.

Taos doesn't look like Santa Fe. It's the worn-out cousin with too many kids and who has time to clean. A tipsy swagger. The Mountain. Backpacks dropped on a curb. Kimberly drives through cottonwoods. She finds the office. Finally. Then she's given a key.

Her casita in the woods looks like a storybook house. Hansel and Gretel were caged in here. No, they're German that's wrong. This is where slow night fires burn. Tethered horses. Broad brimmed hats. Boots. Blankets. Weed. The smell of weed (or skunk?) floats through the air inside. Kimberly opens her suitcase. She unpacks her laptop, her boots, her clothes. Most of her clothes are black. She had noticed, quick impression, that people wear color in Taos. A long and woven coat, violently colored and bordered, had hung from a woman with shocks of hair knotted up in beads. Her own clothes, limp as shadows, belong in New York, she belongs in New York, no, she's here and it's great. She yanks up all the windows to get rid of the smell of skunk (yes, the smell is skunk) then takes a look at the kitchen. Coffee pot, great. Ice tray, great. View from the kitchen, great. Bounce of the mattress, great. Bathroom tub, great. Huge wooden desk at a window, great. View from that window, great great great. This will be the perfect place to start her journey of solitude, her weeks of writing alone, which is what she wanted, didn't she, yes, she wanted to be alone, she wants to be alone, she does she does she does except that lamp, next to the bed, needs to be moved to the corner. The rug on the floor, no. She'll kill herself on that. She's already slid on it once, walking to check the bathroom. Roll that fucker up. Stuff it in the closet. And buy some glade or a lavender bomb or maybe a full-on gas mask to deal with the smell that wait, how bad is it really, how bad, no, it's not bad at all. There's no internet though. There's internet near the office, a half mile walk up the road, but who needs internet all the time, not her, not her, no way, this time is for self-reflection, self-creation, self-destruct, no, not self-destruct, scratch that, get a grip. Go outside. Clean the car.

She pulls out wads of wrappers, Trident and Snickers mostly, from the cup holder in the console. She holds them against her body, pressing with an elbow, as she stretches the thick rubber strap clamped on the garbage bin lid. Bears knock over the bins. She was told the straps are important, though no real reason to worry, we're live-and-let-live about bears out here and we don't call Fish and Game. She's not afraid of bears. She's seen them in the Bronx Zoo. And one, once, from a distance, while hiking in Wyoming. Tikko carried bear spray, but said, as Kimberly heard, there's no real reason to worry. She breathes in juniper air. God, this air is great. She could live on this air. She wouldn't need to eat, wouldn't need to drink, she'd suck this air in her lungs and that would keep her going. Where's she going. Where. She stands between the garbage bin and the door to her casita. She's trapped on the little path. Trapped by her own dumb mind. No, not dumb. She's not dumb. She's merely ruffled, ruffled is all, by the blanching vision of months on end writing in this casita. With Gretel in a cage, cowboys in a hat, Pepe le Pew stinking up the place but hang on, wait, no, it's three months minus some weeks. That's not months on end. She steps off the little path. She stands in the cottonwood trees. These are the trees she'll see from the desk, the enormous wooden desk. A black dog races by. She hears an owner calling. The black dog runs in circles, huge and rippling circles, that spray up twigs and leaves. Kimberly watches the circles. Then she goes inside. She lies face up on the single bed and stares at the stucco ceiling.

I jump to the Laughing Corpse.

"Kimberly's freaking out." (Me.)

"When does that not happen."

"But what do I do?'

"Nothing. She's the one who wants to write and

"Writing is a life raft."

"Pfff."

"For her it is, I swear. Words are real on a page, they sit there, never lying

"Words lie all the time

"But written down they make a life that Kimberly can see

"Control freak then

"Okay. Whatever it is, she needs to write so how do I how do I

"Shhhh."

He picks up his ukulele and sings to me of strength. "Eyes peeled. Wits kept. Always a noble tongue. This will keep her strong and now my song is done." I make a promise for Kimberly. "Pie crust promise," our mother would say, "easy to make, easy to break," but I make it with adobe. I promise to un-think and un-see and un-do anything that might freak her. I've no idea how to do this, but I hold my adobe promise and the song of the Laughing Corpse as I slide back to the casita.

Kimberly's laptop is open. She has a play on her screen. It starts rehearsal after Taos and there's a few tweaks and touches that need to be done, have to be done, so she puts her head down on the desk and waits for words to show up. The play is about forgiveness. It's close to parts of her real real life and close to real is hard. Kimberly loves writing plays, the dialogue, movement, actors, but, in her real real life, and now she tugs at her hair, her plays get performed, when they're performed, in cash-strapped tiny theatres full of scrappy dysfunction. This is my fault, I think, Kimberly's lack of success. I've taken her time, used up her life, and maybe that's me being braggy, maybe I'm not important, but when I see her sitting, the way she's sitting now, with a thought bubble over her head that contains, in curly letters, the phrases "Why do I bother? Why do I even care?" I start to blame myself.

She puts her hands on the keyboard but her people refuse to talk. She buys some colored light bulbs. Lights a candle. Burns some sage. Still they won't start talking. She sweeps the floor. Stomps her feet. Takes her laptop to the porch. She carries it open in her hands and then, oh this is stupid, a burst of rain comes down. Light, brief, unusual, but enough to wreck her keyboard. At the Taos computer store she learns she'll need a new laptop. It might take a week to ship. Maybe two or more.

"This is the Mountain's test." (Computer guy.)

In Taos people say if the Mountain doesn't like you, you leave. If it likes you, you stay. I can't tell if this Mountain story is serious or a joke but the idea of a Mountain throwing its weight around gives me pause. Kimberly walks to a store that sells notebooks and pencils. At the casita she writes dialogue for her play with a pencil covered in drawings of squiggly red chile strings. She rubs a cactus shaped eraser on words she doesn't like. After three days, surprised she's done, she puts the pencil down. Now there's open space. Now there's what the hell.

Kimberly stretches her arms and looks around the casita. The purpose of this residency, she reminds herself while stretching, is let what comes come. There's no expectation of work to be done, handed in, presented, and so, as she was told, the artists use New Mexico, the sky and light of Taos, to fuel imagination. Yes, imagination. I leap in thrill when she laces her boots and opens the wooden door.

The Mountain rises from the Taos Pueblo. Kimberly pays the entry fee and joins a group with a tour guide. In 1906 the United States took many acres from the Pueblo, including the Mountain and Blue Lake. Blue Lake is a sacred pool of water, like a church or cathedral, and the power of the words "church" and "cathedral" were used to fight Congress for return of the Mountain to the Pueblo. The guide gestures toward a dirt field where the original San Geronimo church stood. During the resistance Pueblo citizens took refuge in the San Geronimo church while it was cannonballed. The cannonballs got stuck in the adobe walls so the wooden roof was burned for entry. Then everyone got killed. The replacement San Geronimo church, the one we see in the plaza, was built in 1850. That church is open to the public. The Mountain and Blue Lake are not.

The tour group scatters apart and Kimberly stays by herself. She thinks about New Mexico, the push of the Spanish, then the States, the war for annexation. We're invaders, she notes, aware that her use of 'we' is born of her own history, father raised in New Jersey, mother raised in Nebraska, O New World, O Westward-ho, O Manifest Destiny, O Conquer It, though there's no avoiding wars, pillage, slaves, rape, at least not now, in Kimberly's mind, and in the eyes of time. I wish her skin was thicker and the flotsam of life didn't enter like ink on a tissue. She puts her hand in the river that flows through the Pueblo like wet silver. She watches the water swirl, flowing around her wrist, then puts the cool hand to her face. She walks toward the empty field where the cannonballed church once stood. We stand near the field, tissue as skin, ears open to silence. We hear a crow. The river. We listen together, not apart, and I notice this, I hold it. Then I hear kids yelling. Kimberly hears them too. Wails and screams of dying kids inside the not-there church. We hear them together, she and I, and the hearing hangs between us, a flicker of a moment, until, oh no, oh no, my adobe promise breaks.

Ash kids swoop from the burned-up church, the not-there burned-up church, and they swarm around us in the field, spinning and laughing and having a time, a grand old time with their stories. Stories of fear and capture, stories of near escape, and they whisper and rustle inside our ears as I try to shut them up. Kimberly ducks through a door.

In the low adobe room we catch our breath in silence. A young woman sits by a table. She breathes from an oxygen tank. There's sticks of sage. Feathers. Cash only. Kimberly buys some feathers. When she steps from the low adobe room she looks for the swarming ash kids. They're gone, no longer swarming, and I see, to my surprise, that she's not entirely pleased.

That night a bear walks by. Kimberly watches him lumber. I invite him in.

I make him a bowl of porridge. He takes the bowl in his paws and slurps it with his tongue. I tell him about the ash kids. I tell him I need love. I tell him I need it from Kimberly. I tell him I'm so lonely I talk to bears.

He looks up from his bowl and stares. I stare back until I know (from a bear grumble) that I should quit with the self-pity and get him more porridge. While he eats his second bowl he tells me (bear grumble) that I'm not really alone. I'm like him, a loner, often feared in error.

"Feared? Why am I feared?"

His bear eyes bore into my deepest being. As this happens I feel a warmth like porridge move through my veins.

"What's feared is invisible heart. Yours must be un-feared. Then you'll have her love. And the strength to fly away." (Wordless bear grumble I understand.)

"How do I un-fear it?"

"It must be shown to Kimberly. It must be held and kissed."

"Oh. Oh but

He slurps from his second bowl and I see he's growing impatient.

"I can't let her see the dungeon mind, I can't, I'm sorry, I can't

The bear puts a paw on my shoulder. Then he lumbers out.

I hold his bowl under running water. Flecks of porridge and bear spit swirl around in the drain. The bear doesn't understand. Kimberly can't be in dungeon mind, I can't bring her there, and oh no, oh no, I forgot to tell him the invisible heart sits as a hat on the Laughing Corpse. I forgot to tell the bear I forgot forgot

I race out of the casita into the dark woods screaming "Bear! Bear!" until I trip over a tree root. I collapse in the dirt and sprawl. I know truth knocks once. I don't know what that means but I hear it in my ears as I beg the night sky to show me the bear's face. The sky says "you're on your own, kiddo." I lie face up in the dirt staring at the sky.

Then I feel the press, it's light and very soft, of a solid not-there paw. "Watch for bears in the mountains." I think of Tikko's note and what he said of stillness. The revealing of self to itself, the hacking of stubborn branches, the endless peeling away, until the bolt of something, wordless can't be spoken.

I get up. I lumber to the casita. Kimberly's at the desk with her squiggly red chile pencil. The bowl of eaten porridge is still in the sink. Instead of drying the bowl Kimberly's chewing on the cactus eraser in deep thought or laziness, I don't know which and I don't care, all I want her to do is look up and love me. She doesn't so I give her a headache. When she swallows Tylenol and crawls under the blanket I jump to dungeon mind.

"I have to bring Kimberly here." (Me to the Laughing Corpse.)

"What?"

"I want her to love me. She has to hold the invisible heart and then she has to kiss it. The bear said

"The bear's an idiot."

"But

He pushes his hat (the invisible heart) more firmly onto his skull.

"Kimberly can't be here. Humans make a mess." (Laughing Corpse.)

"I know I know I know but

"I don't want to see her! She'll bring her important real real life and I don't like real life."

'You don't even know what it is."

"I've heard plenty of stories. You're never happy when you come back. That Kimberly person hurts you and I don't want you hurt. Why can't we carry on? We're perfect as we are."

"I don't feel so perfect."

"Red Girl, listen to me. She wants memory gone. That puts you in danger."

I start to shake and tremble. The Laughing Corpse pulls me toward him, hugging me into his bones.

"And I don't want to lose you. Please, Red Girl, please. Choose me and forget her."

He grabs his jaw with his hands, startled by what he's said.

"I'm sorry, I didn't mean – it's not my choice to make. Make yours wise and make it right, that's all I meant to say." (Laughing Corpse.)

His skull is blazing shame. He tips his hat, bows a bit, then runs away in shadow.

Chapter 9
Call It Yours

Kimberly's on the casita bed curled up in a ball. I want to ask her about the choice but I'm a spill of soup. My chest pounds. My hands shake. Where does memory go? Is self a describable thing? I open my mouth. Nothing. My words are puffs of smoke that make no sense at all. I try again. Puffs. I feel the familiar crush, the heavy gravity weight, that pulled me down as ash. How does memory die? What do I have to do? I taste some fear in my mouth and roll it around on my tongue.

"I'm sorry." (Me as smoke.) "I have to find a voice."

In the morning she wakes up early. It's San Geronimo Feast Day at the Taos Pueblo. I don't know what this means, or what the day will bring, but at sunrise Kimberly and some other residents (two composers, one poet, three painters) wait outside for a truck. The truck belongs to the director of the residency. He grew up in Taos, knows it like his hand, so he drives us, bumping, bumping, on several dirt back roads. When we arrive, sun rising, he tells us where to stand. There will be a running, and the path is marked, don't cross it, by strips of yellow crime tape. A structure of aspen branches, shaped like a kind of cross, marks where the runners start. The running is a ritual, no, it's not a race, and the meaning of the ritual (and everything else today) is by tradition, yes, always kept a secret.

Fog steams from a kiva. It's followed by a body. Men with painted skin wind their way to the branches. Women watch from the roofs, bodies wrapped in blankets. Some of the men are old. Some of them are heavy. All of them are barefoot. The men run tall and one at a time. When they run the roofs get vocal. Lulululululuuuu! I hear each runner's breath as I watch their eyes gaze straight. I glance at Kimberly's face. Her eyes are bright with interest and love of something new. She's taking notes in her head (observe observe observe) so I leave her (getting pulled) to the field of the not-there church. I'm startled to see the ash kids. They drop from the air like petals and swarm around me happy. Then, like a whoosh of tornado, all of them swoop me up. They carry me through their years of forgetting and un-forgetting, forgetting and un-forgetting, as they rustle and whisper their stories. I strain my ears to hear, I want to catch the words, and when they drop me to the ground many hours have passed.

Kimberly's now at a door. She stands with the other residents talking and waiting and waiting. The clowns appear when they're ready, and not a moment before, according to the gray-haired man who's also waiting. He tells us the door leads to his family's Pueblo home. It's rarely used these days, they come for festivals only, but, and we might like to know this, he's the keeper of the drum. A composer in our group points her finger at something. He raps her hand, flirting.

"It's not okay to point here." (Keeper of the drum.)

He shows a quick nudge with his chin.

"That's the way we point."

"Means 'hey fuck off' in Manhattan." (Kimberly joking around.)

The drum keeper laughs a rolling laugh as Kimberly looks at the plaza. Maybe she'll write his laugh someday (she's thinking this to herself) when suddenly, loud and blaring, the clowns burst out from nowhere.

Their naked skin is painted with stripes of black and white. Their hair is pointed spikes. Their job is chaos, making fear, and they scoop up kids and toss them or dunk them into the river. They yank off hats from heads and hold them out for money. They put a cop in handcuffs. They sit in a circle and smoke while chomping down on melons. I see a small girl cry. I want a clown to dunk me so I can scream underwater, head all wet and drowning, "I'm not scared of you!" I'm never scared, ever, Red Girl's never scared, and I say this lie to a clown, the one who's chomping melon, while he spits his seeds in the dirt.

The clowns stick around for an hour, or maybe more, I don't know, but when they're done with their chaos I stand in front of Kimberly (she still can't see me with her) and I pull myself up tall. I tell her I live in a dungeon mind at the bottom of her being. I tell her she'll love it there. I tell her I'll perch on a sacrifice ledge and die for her if she wants.

She drinks an instant coffee then wanders around the plaza. Turquoise. Silver. Blankets. She looks at some, doesn't buy, and then, at last, finally, the clown men appear again. They walk barefoot toward a log that's stripped and set in the dirt. It stands in the dirt as a very tall pole and from its top, very high, hang two bags of harvest and one dead sheep.

The men look at the pole. They look at the bags and dead sheep. The goal is to reach the top. The first several men race toward the pole. They use nothing but bare hands and bare feet to climb. The ground below is hard, a fall could bring you death, and I watch them drop with exhaustion. Then a young man screams. He hurls himself at the pole and the crowd shouts as his muscles jump and his body, climbing, climbing, creeps its way up higher, higher to the top. From there he cuts a bag that hangs.

Drops it. Cuts the other. The final cut is the hung dead sheep. Red dust flies when the sheep falls down, flying, thud, to its back.

He sits on the pole up high. He raises his arms. Screams to the sky. My heart starts pounding pounding. (Life atop a pole. Scream! Call it yours!) After his echo fades he lets his body loosen. He swings his feet, drops his arms, gazes straight ahead. The ash kids rustle my ears (Scream! Call it yours!) while I turn my eyes away.

The drum keeper holds aspen branches.

"We pull the aspen structure down, then keep a branch for luck. The luck will last a year." (Drum keeper.)

He gives a branch to Kimberly. The sun sinks toward the ground. Driving back in the truck we see a running horse. It's beautiful, gray, racing, a mane of quivering strings. At the casita, on her desk, Kimberly lays out the aspen branch. I touch the leaves. I run barefoot. I climb the high pole and scream. I ride the gray horse to my sacrifice ledge and look at the crowd that yawns. I don't call for Kimberly. I don't wait for an answer. I know what I have to do.

Chapter 10
Waking

3:00 a.m. on her iPhone. I look at Kimberly's sleeping cheek and press myself through time. The un-forgetting. Years ago. Knobby-kneed girl. Streak of blood. Translucent as a hologram but very very real. Can I be that again? Can I?

I wave my arms in front of my eyes and see a flutter of ghost. Kimberly must be dreaming. She must want this too. I tell her (wordless still) what little I know of brain. A brain can be handed to a man of straw (Wizard of Oz.) It can be turned into a soccer ball to kick around (Mayan.) It can be served on a plate (French cuisine.) It can be drilled with holes or given shocks. I don't know where free will is located, or ethics, decision, art, science, math, violin playing, chess winning, joke telling, love of dogs, hate of fleas, but I think scientists can look at the brain and poke places that light up. I don't know if I'd light up. I don't know where I spark in brain, translucent girl that I am. All I know is I'm sorry.

"Kimberly." (Smokeless whisper.)

"Nah No Wha?"

She sits up in the dark and waves a stop-it hand. She turns on a lamp that shines pink from the colored light bulb she bought at Walmart. She walks to the kitchen (I follow) and pours a glass of gin. She holds the glass for a long long time then turns to me, eyes puffy, and spills the gin on the floor. She pulls a cushion from the kitchen chair. She yells into the cushion. When she's done yelling she puts the cushion down and gets a paper towel. She kneels on the kitchen floor, dabbing up the gin. Then she looks at me.

"What are you doing." (Kimberly.)

"Please un-fear the invisible heart."

"Invisible heart? What?"

"Where we split in two. The bear says

Kimberly crushes the paper towel and heads back to the sink. She pours a new glass of gin and adds some tonic water. She cuts lime with a stabbing motion to show she's nearing her rope end then sips her drink slowly. When she's halfway done she looks over the glass.

"I'm not listening to a made-up bear." (Kimberly.)

"He's not made-up he's

Kimberly shoots rays from her face. I shoot back.

"He asked for nothing but two bowls of porridge for the deepest truth."

"Oh Red Girl, oh oh oh

Kimberly slides to the floor, now sitting low with me.

"What's the deepest truth?" (Kimberly.)

"I live in a secret world. I'm trapped and I can't fly."

Kimberly's eyes go soft. I speak to her again.

"If you un-fear the invisible heart, if you hold and kiss it, we'll see elusive love. Then I can fly away. I can leave you alone forever."

Kimberly laughs a cynical laugh.

"You mean like dying?"

"Yes."

"And you're willing to do that for me?"

I nod my little head. Kimberly dabs her eyes.

"Thank you Red Girl."

"Yes."

We sit on the floor in silence. The wall clock ticks. The gin lime bobs. Kimberly (I can see it) wonders if she's cracking. I touch her leg in comfort.

"I think you called me here. I don't think you're cracking." (Me.)

I know why she fears the cracking. I used to make her crazy. I pulled her into flashbacks, endless no-noise screams, endless un-forgettings, endless cycles of real/not real but I promise her now (in silence) that I won't do that again. This time I'll be leaving. This time I can die. She can trust me (trust me, please) to fly away for good.

"I'm scared of your secret world." (Kimberly looking scared.)

"You don't have to be scared. The invisible heart is there. Everything is there. It's a beautiful place. It's a church of you. I made it to protect us and if you see it, if you come, I promise you will love it."

Kimberly downs her gin and puts the glass on the floor.

"Okay. Let's go."

"Oh. I can jump back and forth, but you? I'm not sure how. Try your hands on knees. Maybe like meditation."

She crosses her ankles on the floor. She breathes slowly, hands on knees, draining much of her thought. I watch her eyes go quiet. I see a flicker of self drift away from her body. I gently, very gently, open a gauze that hides. I walk her down the steps. Dark moss. Dust. She follows slowly (steps are steep) till we reach a pile of papers.

"These are pages of all you've read and over the years forgotten." (Me.)

Kimberly picks up pages. Shakespeare, Plato, Blake, Bronte, Austen, Woolf, and so many, so many others. A million poets and fairy tales, a million children's stories, and a few torn pages in French when she could still speak French.

"I read all this?"

"I think so."

"That's a lot to read. And sure is a lot to forget."

"That's why I keep the pages. Just in case, you know?"

"In case what?"

I shrug. I really have no idea. Kimberly's eyes perk open. She races toward the path that leads to Wisp's old tree.

"Look look look! These are beautiful stones!"

I try to stop her from touching but Kimberly picks up lava stones and dribbles them through her hands. They slip like a river of pearls, purple, green, red, until she grips them hard.

"What the fuck are these?" (Kimberly.)

"Put them down."

"No! Get the hell away from me, don't touch me, don't you touch

I move to pull a pearl from her hand and she smacks me across the face.

"I told you not to touch me!"

"These are stones of anger. Throw them from your hands."

"Don't tell me what to do. Little bitch. Fuckwad. Get out of my way you shit."

She clomps her feet as she walks the path. I jump up into her arms to pry her fingers open. She yells and shakes me loose. I grab her by the ankles and she goes splat on the path, cursing me like a witch, a witch who's gone deranged, so I hold her down and sit on her spine and whack her fists till they open. When the last pearl spills to the ground I climb from her back, gather the pearls, then lay them down on the path. Kimberly follows behind me. I turn to her when I'm done and her face looks swirly large.

"What the hell?" (Kimberly.)

"I know I know I know

"What are those?"

"All your anger. I polish them into pearl but they still pack a punch. I'm used to it, I can touch them, but you should stay away."

"You hurt my back."

"I'm sorry. It's years and years of anger, yours and mine together, so I thought I better

"Yeah

"Nip it in the

"Yeah yeah yeah."

Kimberly takes a breath and exhales like a tire. Then she shakes her hands, rolls her head in a circle, and massages both of her shoulders. I point to the sacrifice ledge.

"That's where I die for the good of all." (Me.)

"Great. Let's take a look."

We struggle up the steps (she's the one who's winded) until we're at the top. From the top she looks at throngs while I go all Oh and dance-y. Then she waves her hand.

"What are you doing?" (Me.)

"Waving to our family."

"There's no humans here!"

"I see mom and Eliza and Aunt Louise and Uncle Rob and

"No! No! No! You're not allowed to be here if you're going to go all real."

"But

"Everything here is true and right and none of it is literal."

"But what if I see

"You don't. Not here. Not ever. No."

"Okay, Red Girl. Wow, okay."

"I'm sorry but I

"Yeah, I know. I get it. I understand."

Kimberly's pretty miffed (her smile doesn't fool me) but she follows me down the sacrifice ledge then stops as if she's been struck. She stares at the girl-at-her-desk. She waves her hand in front of the girl but of course the girl stays still.

"Why is she frozen?" (Kimberly.)

"She's always been like that."

Kimberly touches the golden squirrel.

"He was a book report prize. We won him in second grade and oh, wait, can I say that? I don't want to be literal but

"I already know what he is."

She pokes his empty eye then pulls out a bit of lint.

"She's frozen in Los Angeles." (Kimberly.) "The memories there were strange, so maybe that's why she's

"I don't care. We're not here for her."

Kimberly puts the squirrel down. She wants to stay all nicety-nice so she stands him on his pin and makes him talk to the girl-at-her-desk in a stupid squeaky voice.

"Red Girl's right, she's always right. We're not here for you. We're here for invisible heart."

"Knock that off."

"Come on. You're acting really snotty

"I'm scared, all right? I'm nervous."

"Well so am I

"Okay. Let me just -- okay. I have to tell you something."

Kimberly sits on a stone (not a lava stone) and folds her hands in her lap. I say I'm grateful to have her here, I'm grateful, I'm so very grateful, that she's giving me her attention, this full and true attention, and what I have to say is, well, it's kind of wordless, but I'll do my best to put my words on what is invisible heart.

Kimberly gives me a look.

"Get on with it, would you?"

"I'm trying. The invisible heart is formless. It has no shape or circumference. It's a miracle. It's an event. It's where we split in two when there seemed no other choice. But here, and this is the challenge, it's a hat on the Laughing Corpse."

Kimberly's eyes go hooded. She tries to stay all open (her effort is palpably clear) but she's also a person who doesn't love, in fact she intensely dislikes, new unexpected facts.

"He wears the invisible heart to protect me from its weight. It's a terrible burden, all that blame and fear, so after you un-forgot he offered to hold it forever. He won't want you to have it. He thinks you're a dangerous thing for me, and said, though he took it back, that I should choose him not you."

"Sounds like kind of a jerk."

"No no no, he's love itself! Look what he gave me for you."

I lift up my hair and show her the bone.

"I touched you with this in Chimayo. Remember that feeling of calm? It came from this finger bone. A broken piece of himself that he gave to me for protection. All he wants to do, ever ever ever, is give us his protection. That's what love is, right?"

"Um, well

"Yes! When I feel bad and horrible his bones are soft and deep. They're the place, the only place, where I'm safe and alive and protected and don't have to oh, oh no no

I've started to choke with tears. I pull myself together, not wanting Kimberly's pity.

"I still get tears, I'm sorry, when I think of the Laughing Corpse. After your birthday burn his bones were scattered and lost. I wandered alone in the dark, this whole place was dark, and I picked through all the wreckage. I lifted bone after bone, threading him back together, until, on the stone where you're sitting, I found his severed skull. He still wore the invisible heart. He hadn't let it go. That's loyalty. That's love. He'll never stop protecting me so let me do the talking. I mean when he shows up."

I call for the Laughing Corpse. He doesn't know Kimberly's here and this makes me very shaky. My voice goes warbly high as I call and call and call for him and Kimberly drums her fingers. Finally I see him walking. His hands are trembling slightly as they cover his socket eyes.

"You've brought her here." (Laughing Corpse.)

"Yes, I made the choice."

I see his shoulders shake while his hands still cover his sockets.

"Don't make me see you old. I think that could kill me." (Laughing Corpse.)

"Wow that's pretty rich, coming from a skeleton." (Kimberly getting pissed.)

The Laughing Corpse drops his hands.

"Call it the shock of disgust."

"At what. Age? Time?"

"At the wish to kill our Red Girl for the sake of an idiot bear."

"He's not an idiot bear." (Me trying to get control.) "He talked to me, I heard him, and he knows what Kimberly wants. She wants to love me, that's what I think, and she and I can't go on like this, split in two like a cracked-up nut and

"Why can't you go on?"

"Because

And then I stop. I can't explain the bear. I can't explain the reason. My whole life is unexplained as I come and go, rise and fall, torture, comfort, make a self, make a story of life that Kimberly seems to control, but maybe not, it might be me, we fight ourselves, we push and pull, and I'm so tired of fighting, tired of needing and wanting, tired of getting blamed, tired of seeing the Laughing Corpse, tired of being stretched, and I'm stretched between them now, I see myself like gum, a twiny twisty thing held by her and held by him and stretched and stretched and stretched until I'm about to snap.

"I want to leave. It's my choice. Give her invisible heart." (Me.)

"I never said I wouldn't."

The Laughing Corpse lowers his head, bowing now to Kimberly as if she's some kind of queen. She looks at me. I look at her. Then she touches his hat. She tries to pull it from his head but it won't move an inch. I grab one side of his hat, she holds tight to the other, and together we yank and yank.

"It's in like a tick." (Kimberly.)

The Laughing Corpse does a handstand while shaking his head back and forth. This doesn't loosen invisible heart so I start to feel a panic. I can't control the dungeon mind, I don't know why, I don't know why, it must be Kimberly's presence, it must be Kimberly's face, I want so much to please her and now, oh now now now

Title of Book: _Help!_

Kimberly yells at the Laughing Corpse.

"You're keeping her trapped on purpose!" (Kimberly.)

"I swear I'm not, I swear

"Then give her what she wants!"

The Laughing Corpse goes all dramatic and knocks his head on a stone. He's trying to dislodge the invisible heart so he knocks it over and over. The noise of his head against the stone pops like the shot of a rifle. Bang bang bang, louder louder louder, while Kimberly wails like a crow gone mad with "Liar! Liar! Liar!"

Then a pencil cracks.

The girl-at-her-desk stands up. Her eyes shine. Her skin glows.

"I'm trying to write a book report. Please stop making noise." (Girl-at-her-desk.)

She pulls a new pencil from her desk. She walks (with very stiff legs) over the stones to Kimberly.

"You can un-fear with this." (Girl-at-her-desk to Kimberly.)

Kimberly takes the pencil. Her voice is soft and hoarse.

"Do you mean write the invisible heart?" (Kimberly.)

"That's the way to un-fear it. You'll hold and kiss the words. You won't need him at all."

The Laughing Corpse lets out a cry.

"No, no, no. There were threats, knives, drowning if you tell. Drop the pencil. Drop it. Don't write the invisible heart." (Laughing Corpse.)

Kimberly takes his bony hand and stares in his socket eyes. Something flickers between them. Cold, hot, cold. I feel myself expand as the two of them, now as giants, pull my life like string.

"I know what you are." (Kimberly.)

The Laughing Corpse steps away.

"You're Red Girl's love and strength. Let her do what's right."

The Laughing Corpse touches my head, checks my hair for the bone, then presses me, very lightly, on the tips of my shoulder blades.

"Yes. Do what's right." (Laughing Corpse to me.)

He leaves and we're alone. Kimberly holds the pencil then pokes her palm with the point. She looks at the little mark on her hand then closes her eyes, squeezing, clearly trying to think. I wait for her to finish. When she does she looks at me as if from on a ceiling.

"I can't write our story. I lived it from a distance. Out of my body, out of my skin, and here's what I would write: 'Kimberly recalled dissociated memories at age thirty-seven. The end.'" (Kimberly.)

I laugh at this. Kimberly laughs too. Then she gives me a not-on-the-ceiling look so real I almost faint.

"You're the one to write it." (Kimberly.)

"But but but but but

She hands me the wooden pencil. She picks me up then puts me down. I'm startled to see the casita desk. I press myself in Kimberly's chair and stare through the pane glass window. I see the cottonwood trees. I see the black dog running. I speak to my fear in a whisper. "This is like a book report. The story's already made so I can't get in trouble."

Chapter 11
Writing

I write the very first words. "I hang like a fool in the sky."

Then I write of falling as ash, the starting in Los Angeles, my pull to the car, my dungeon mind, my missing Little One, Lola, Wisp, the meeting with Laughing Corpse. I write to the end of this sentence and now, in the casita, I worry about my facts.

I want to write the facts but there's no way, no way, to sift with true precision. I think about the bear. I tell myself I'm a single tree falling unheard in the woods. The bear will lumber through the trees and perk up his round bear ears. His ears will make me loved because I am, I know I am, but all my life they've turned away, the ears I want to hear, the heads I want to nod, so how do I do it, how do I fact, how do I how do I

Stop.

Title of Book: _Red Girl Jumping_.

True Fact In The Book: _a) The book report prize of a golden squirrel. b) Captain Grammar and no-noise screams. c) The un-forgetting in year thirty-seven. d) Little One, Wisp, Lola. e) Kimberly's family. f) The estrangement. g) Kimberly burning the papers of un-_

forgetting on her year fifty birthday h) Kimberly driving to Santa Fe with Tikko. i) me writing in the casita.

Favorite Part: _Nubs of wings breaking through my back._

Least Favorite Part: _Dying._

I look at the casita window. Kimberly's in the kitchen making a pot of coffee. I call to her (she won't answer) then step outside in the dark. The stars are bright and alive as I raise my face to New Mexico sky then press myself through time. I call for Little One, Lola, Wisp (I really really need them) until, I can't believe it, three ashes petal down.

I put my fingers to my lips, warning them to whisper.

"I'm writing invisible heart." (Me.)

"About fucking time, don't you think?" (Lola.) "Kimberly and her boxes, labelled with that "Someday," has been dragging her ass for years."

"Why can't she write it herself?" (Wisp.)

"She was barely there. That's why I need your help."

"She won't want others hurt. Use her name. Use our names. Change the names of others. Then stay as true as you can." (Wisp.)

"Like that ever means a thing." (Lola.)

"It might this time." (Me.)

"I go first." (Little One.) "I'm the youngest here."

Little One opens the wooden door as all of us jump in surprise. We follow her to the casita desk (I check if Kimberly's watching) where she holds out her hand, ready, impatient for the pencil.

"You don't have to help me. I'll do this by myself." (Little One.)

Chapter 12
Little One

I'm Little One. I'm year four to eight.

I like to hide in closets. I don't like to exist. If I have to talk I pretend I'm an echo. In the closet I hide in back. I tie up Daddy's laces. I put my hands in toe shoes. Mommy doesn't dance now. She still keeps the shoes. I hear her voice from the closet. I hear Daddy's too. Whatever I touch in the closet makes me not exist.

Outside I ride a trike. One day a person breaks it. I don't see that happen. I see the metal twisted. Mommy says too bad. Maybe I'll have a new one if money grows on trees. Then it's time for snow. In Wisconsin snow is radioactive. Don't eat snow. Ever. I eat snow. I don't explode. I never lick a bike rack. There's a boy who did. His tongue got froze to the rack and they had to cut it off. One day Eliza sinks in snow. Her head sticks out. She calls for help. I see my boots run fast. I find Mommy. She lifts her up. It leaves a hole in the snow.

When I walk to kindergarten I pass a path in the woods. Devils and monsters use the path. I run it once on a dare. Boys can pull your pants down. Break a robin's egg. I don't like the path. I like swings. I walk to the swings every day. I climb the metal pole. I sit up high on top. I'm not allowed to sit there. I can sit in the cloth seat. I can aim for the top of trees. I can leap and fall in the dirt. I can lie on my back and watch the sky. When I'm dizzy birds fly backward.

Daddy comes to get me. He hangs me on a monkey bar. He pokes a thumb in privates. I like that don't I. Don't I. My hands get cold on the monkey bar but I'm a strong little thing. I go to the sky with birds. I have a beak. I eat a worm. I fly backward in the sky. After I leave the sky Daddy lifts me up. He puts me on his shoulders. I'm high up here. I'm high. I grab his forehead happy. He tells me I'm safe. Don't worry. He skips a bit to scare me. At home he holds my ankles. I get spun real fast. I scream when the carpet nears my face. Do it again! Fly me! Mommy says watch out. Time to stop right now.

At bedtime he tells stories. Pirates and headless ghosts. Dire doom is everywhere and the stories end on the plank. To be continued. Finish it now! That's me and Jim and Eliza. We whisper together in bed. We dream of falling in water. Oceans full of pirates. Sharks who swallow kids.

Once we drive to Nebraska. Mommy's daddy and mommy live in a house with a porch swing. Mommy's daddy was a mail man. Now he has false teeth. He claps them at us. You git out! Grandma says he's jokin'. Don't you mind that man. Grasshoppers are poison. That's what the false teeth say. If their juice gets on your skin you die a poison death. Jim and Eliza and I sit by an open field. Grasshoppers jump. The whole field jumps. We're afraid to cross. We hold each other's hands. We run it fast and live. Now we know. Now we know. Jokes can be a lie.

In Wisconsin Mommy flattens pie crust. To make the dough she squishes butter in her hands. Her mommy in Nebraska uses hands. That's the way. Not two forks. When Mommy puts crust on a pan the edges hang over. She trims the edges with a knife. I can take the trims. I mold stars of dough. I sprinkle cinnamon on. My stars come out of the oven and race across the pan. I eat a star. It makes me brave. I tell Mommy about the thumb. Why does she call it my private part. Daddy says it's his. Mommy slaps my face. The star breaks in my mouth. Nothing's real. I'm not real. I don't like to exist.

Daddy says I do. Daddy says I exist so much I make him do things. Things I really like. I like it don't I. Don't I. I like to be a bird. I like to fly in the sky.

Mommy forgets the slap. She lets me eat more stars and spread the crayons out. I have to share the crayon box with Eliza and Jim. I like Eliza and Jim but they always dull the points. I want my own box with the extra colors. I sit on Santa's lap and ask for the box of crayons. Mommy says don't do that. I make us sound real poor. When Easter comes we hold a wire. It fits around an egg. You hold the wire. You dip the egg in hot color. You stripe the egg if you want. The egg cools down. You get a crayon. You draw a face on the egg. After Easter you peel off the face. You eat blue and red egg salad. You're a cannibal.

One day Daddy wears a gown with a square on top of his head. Eliza and Jim and Mommy and I watch him in a crowd. He gets a rolled up paper. People clap when he gets it. Words get printed on paper. Paper makes them real. I start to look at words. I take them in the closet.

After the rolled up paper we move. We live in a house that grows from a hill. Pepe next door has a goat. I ask for a goat. No goat. Maybe a dog if I'm good. I don't walk to school. I wait down the hill for a bus. In first grade there's a rooster. The teacher tells us touch his comb. I'm good so I get to go first. Daddy's a teacher too. He rides a bike to school. The name is only letters. U and C and L and A. In swimming pools we ride his back. Eliza and Jim and I cling and hold on tight. Then we're thrown like comets. We scream till our throats give out. More!

Give us more! He throws us again. One more time. Then again and again.

I'm good so we get a dog. The dogs all bark in cages. One dog doesn't bark. Eliza and Jim and I say that's the one. She's the one. She's black and white with floppy ears. Those are my favorite ears. In the car she sits in my lap. Her weight is perfect. Fur is smooth. The name on her tag is Susie.

Susie lives on a leash outside. When she's not on her leash she's in the house with Jim and Eliza and me. We tie her to piles of indoor things we want to watch fall down. Eliza puts a bone near her mouth. Jim makes the tower of things. I pet her fur. When she goes for the bone everything falls down and we do it again. We love Susie. She never bites or snaps. She only licks our skin.

One day she's gone. Her leash is all chewed up. Every day after school I run from the bus to our house. I yell out Susie's name. I know she's up the hill. I know she's caught in branches. I know she's starving. At night I cry in my bed. I want to die. I want to be Astroboy. I sit up in my bed. I can be Astroboy. Astroboy is a cartoon who has jets in his feet and two pointed black spikes for hair. I wet my hair. I make it two points. I run and blast off. I fly up over the hills. My eye beams see the tree tops. I use all my power. I send a message to Susie. Come home! Come back! Run! The next day she runs down the hill. Her breath is hot. I see her ribs. Her tongue is lapping fast. I put my face in her fur. I can't believe. I leap inside. Astroboy is magic. Now I'm magic too.

I'm not magic every day. Maybe once a week. I keep the magic secret. If anyone knew my power I'd be eaten alive. I control the world. I control what happens. I'm the reason we move. My parents think it's them but I know the truth of magic. Magic makes me fly. Magic makes my Daddy. Magic makes us move.

The new house doesn't grow from a hill. It sits by a parking lot. In the new house I write book reports. I walk to Beverly Vista school. My socks flutter down. I pull them up. At Beverly Vista school there are girls who have socks that stay up. Their shoes match dresses. I go to Goodwill for dresses. Daddy has no Oscar. Mommy rolls dough. No TV. Read a book. I stand by myself at recess. I bite my nails to blood.

Miss Fern holds up a picture. This is Chagall. There is a cow that floats in a face and a person in the sky. She asks if the picture can be real. I think the picture is a dream that's real. I want to raise my hand. I can't. Miss Fern holds me like chalk. I powder. Leave white dust. I fly out windows. Hover. Touch my beak to the pane. I see chalk children. I see me. Pale. Shaking hand. Miss Fern taps me at recess. "You can be my helper. New friends will go to your desk."

New friends who are not my friends line up at my desk. I tell them what I know. I know three plus five. I know reading. I know holding a pencil. I don't tell them what else I know. I know I'm a girl with the body of a bird at the window. I know Astroboy can't save Eliza. I know Chagall can't. Eliza is strapped to tables. She is having her skin pricked. She is living in a whiteness. There are walls. Rules. Doctors. Children are not allowed to visit the hospital. It's dangerous. If it's dangerous why is Eliza there? Mommy doesn't know. No one knows. Eliza is trapped in a whiteness because she woke up and couldn't move. She couldn't walk. She couldn't lift her head. She could whisper "I'm frozen." My magic sends her safety thoughts. Come home. Come back. Stay alive. I write a thousand book reports. I win the golden squirrel. I tell the squirrel to save Eliza. He can take his missing eye to her bedside. He can skitter up a tree and race down the halls of the hospital. He can drop his ruby eye in jello which they will feed her. She will swallow the eye jewel. She will come back to life. She will rise up out of her white sheet and say "Where is my sister? I want to see my sister!" The golden squirrel will put her on his back and fly out the window. Guards and doctors and rules will fall down like plastic soldiers when Jim makes a war.

My magic doesn't work. Every night Mommy comes home from the hospital saying no news. Daddy makes friends with people who feel sorry for us. One man brings a bucket of fried chicken. We don't eat bucket chicken. We eat vegetables. I tip the bucket to rain the crumbs and the man who brought them laughs. Then he touches my hair.

Magic makes me twirl. Magic makes me dance. Magic makes me lie on the floor for Daddy's friends. Magic makes them drink. Magic makes them water me like a plant. Magic makes them push me up and down. Magic makes them laugh. Magic makes Mommy stay at the hospital. Magic makes her not see. Magic makes a blue van pick me up. Magic makes the blue van drive me to a mansion in the Hollywood hills. Magic makes a large swimming pool in the mansion. Magic makes everyone swim naked. Magic makes girls and grownups swim together. Magic makes a round bed. Magic makes a man come in. Magic makes another man. Magic makes another man. Magic makes a camera watching. Magic makes a man take us to a cliff. Magic makes the man tell us to say we went horseback riding. Magic makes the man say he will cut off our arms and legs and throw us over the cliff into the ocean if we don't say horseback riding.

Magic makes me forget this. Magic makes the blue van and cliff and Daddy's friends and flying backward roll into dark clouds. Magic makes the dark clouds roll to a darker place where a small girl stands on a ledge. Magic makes her take the clouds. Magic makes her eat them. I don't know she's Red Girl. I don't know that yet.

One day Mommy says Eliza can come home. The doctors who keep her trapped don't know why she froze. No one knows why it happened. I know why it happened. I didn't take good care. I'll watch Eliza like an owl. I'll never shut my eyes. I'll keep her in my sight and blast off every danger. When she comes home she's quiet. I want to hug her. I want to eat her. I want to tell her how hard the golden squirrel and I cried out for her. How thick the walls. How white. I don't tell her. Our family is jokes. Books. Don't-say-it.

Miss Fern tells Mommy I can skip third grade. Fourth grade is giants. They'll rip my arms off and say fe fi fo fum. I hold my breath till I can't. Then I blow out the breath and it swirls over the ocean and makes a wave that washes to another side of the world where Daddy gets a Fulbright. The Fulbright pulls us out of Los Angeles. It is true magic. I will go to third grade in Andernos, France.

Before we go I learn Je m'appelle Kimberlie and Ou est la ou le _____? Also Ecole Chat Chien and

Kim Merrill

Lundi Mardi Mecredi Jeudi Vendredi Samedi Dimanche. Eliza and Jim and I get shots and passports. We ride a boat that leaves from New York City. From the boat we wave to Daddy's mommy. She lives in a red tower on 14th Street and Avenue C. I don't cry because we will see Susie again in one year.

We ride the boat for five days. It has a swimming pool of salt water. It has a playroom. It has a deck with chairs on it. When I stand on the deck I see pirates underwater. One has a knife in his mouth. He puts a finger on his lips. Shhhhh. Don't tell. I want to ask how he keeps his hat on underwater. I don't ask. I like pirate stories but I don't want to walk the plank. I look around the deck. Maybe they'll choose the lady in a wheelchair. She's old and won't mind. What if they want kids? For easier chewing. There's a lot of kids on the boat. One is a girl with shriveled arms. She hits a ball with her chest. She looks at us with "So? I know I'm flippered." I ask Mommy why she's flippered. Thalidomide. Thalidomide was prescribed if you were pregnant and felt sick. Now it's against the law. If the flipper girl is against the law she can walk the plank. Then I stop. I hate myself. It's not the fault of the flipper girl. I should walk the plank. I should lean over the railing and say "take me." I start to lean but Jim walks up behind me. He pinches my arm. Time to eat.

We sit at a round table in the children's dining room. There is a tablecloth and heavy silverware. A waiter with a towel over his arm serves hot food. When he lifts the dome I see a pirate hook. I blink. I see an omelet. I understand the sea. Things live underneath. People bob on top. I want to be an octopus. I want to dive to the bottom and hit the murk. I want to watch it rise. I want to shoot out ink.

In Andernos the ocean is near. We walk to salty flats. There are bubbles of clams and crayfish. Muck that sucks your feet. I'm careful on the seaweed. Seaweed covers holes that lead to a deep lair. In the lair are blood sucking octopuses who live on dead pirates. They like pirates but their favorite food is English-speaking kids. I am careful on the seaweed because Eliza and Jim and I are the only English-speaking kids in the town.

If I do get sucked in I will speak French. I know more words. Croissant. Pain Chocolate. Gribouille. Gribouille means stupid. The teacher says gribouille. We call her Madame. Gribouiller is the verb of gribouille. It means scribble. In Andernos we sit at wooden desks for two people. On the top corners of the desk are two wells of purple ink. We dip pens in. We write letters that go straight up and down instead of slant. We practice strings of each letter on lines in our cahiers. If the ink pen blobs it shoots purple spiders on the page. These are gribouilles. They are very bad. I get called gribouille. When it happens I get tears in my eyes. I stare at the dirty neck of Pascal in front of me. He doesn't care about gribouilles. He laughs when Madame hits his head.

Behind our house is a train track. When I hear the whistle I climb the fence to practice magic. I jump in front of the train. I hold my hands out to push the engine. I have to save a rabbit who is chewing grass on the track. I push and push and push to shove the train away. I watch it roll backward. I wipe my greasy hands. In France they eat rabbits. I eat a rabbit at school lunch. When I find out I cough up fur for days.

One day I see Mommy in the kitchen. She holds a big chicken upside down. It has no feathers but has a head. Mommy says the chicken has all of its guts inside. She doesn't want to pull the guts out. She can't. Her daddy twisted the necks of chickens in the backyard of Nebraska. She doesn't want to remember that. She wants a clean chicken from a store in America. When she stops crying she makes crepes suzette. She flips the thin batter and sets it on fire. She loves French cooking. She's sorry about the crying. Next time she'll know. She'll say "gut the poulet." In the morning she sleeps late. I walk to the bakery and say "Deux croissants et trois pain chocolats." I carry them home in a paper bag. Mommy cries when she sees them. She's happy I got the breakfast. She's so very tired.

Daddy gets fat eating pastries. After school he meets Jim and Eliza and me at the creek on our way home. He brings paper and folds boats. We float them on the creek. I push mine with a stick and drown an entire family. The old men who play Bocce ball don't hear the cries. After the creek is the pastry store. We buy éclairs. We say "Gluttony is a sin we gladly commit." At the Andernos house the Seven Deadly Sins hang in picture frames. I pass Gluttony Sloth Wrath Greed Pride Lust and Envy as I climb the stairs to my room. The Seven Sins are going to hell. There's fire around their feet. In my room is a bed with a dark headboard. The headboard is huge and carved. When I have to fly backward and then forget I dive through the carved dark wood. I wander in a forest. I peck carved wood with my beak.

The house is full of dark wood. At the foot of the stairs is a gray marble head of a child. I touch his curls sometimes. They are cold with a little dust. The house creaks with sound but it's not haunted. I know this because I check. I open every drawer. I lift the Deadly Sins. I punch through all the pillows. I unscrew jars of jam. There's nothing in the cellar. It might not be a cellar. An eyeball is a grape. A noose blown rope. Blood on the floor is wine. I tell Eliza and Jim we are safe. They look at me like I'm gribouille. They know they're safe. They haven't asked. They go back to Bob and Bob. Bob and Bob are two walking fingers. They have the same name because Eliza and Jim are too gribouille to think of a different one. All Bob and Bob do is fight fires. They walk up the ladder of the plastic fire truck and kick pennies away. Bob and Bob are boring. I say this to Eliza and Jim. They don't care.

Eliza and Jim go to the same classroom. They have a teacher who speaks some English. They're not alone in a sea of bobbing words that make no sense. In Los Angeles I won a book report prize. I wasn't a slow girl who had to cheat. I never made mistakes. If I did I scratched them out. I had a pink eraser. I can't erase gribouilles. I want to use a pencil. I scream these things in the kitchen. Mommy says calm down. I'm having a big adventure. Some day I'll look back.

I do homework from the Ecole grammar book. Underneath a noun is a red square. Under a verb is a blue triangle. Under an object noun is a green circle. A red square does a blue triangle to a green circle. Daddy helps me learn this. We sit against my dark headboard and I hold the grammar book. I start to see that words do the same thing in French as they do in English. A sentence is a string of shapes. Words are shapes. Words are alive. One day at school I understand everything. I write stories in French. I have no gribouilles. I have Bon! Tres Bien! Charmant! I am in French heaven. I twirl berets. I suck Gauloises. I fall into soft baguettes.

In our cahier we copy pictures from our history book. I draw Joan D'Arc who looks at the sky while burning. Les Etats Unis doesn't exist in the book until halfway through. Then it's a fur source for trappers. There are no kings or martyrs or guillotines in Les Etats Unis.

I draw a Coat of Arms. I want a D' in my name like the man in the castle. I look around the classroom. Pascal doesn't have a D'. Neither does my desk mate. We look like the dwarfs and serfs who pull the wooden carts. Pascal calls me Cold Cut. "C'est ca toi!" I don't understand so I ask him. "Do you mean full of baloney?" "Oui! C'est ca! Les Americains sont betes!" In the cement yard kids circle Eliza and Jim and me. They chant "betes betes betes!" Then we play chase. I trip and fly in the air. I land on top of my head. I stand up. I shove Pascal. In the schoolroom letters in my cahier float like purple threads in water. My head pounds. I might throw up. On our walk home Daddy meets us by the creek. He sees my dizzy face and swings me up to safety. Finally I can cry. I'm carried home. Put to bed. I miss a week of school.

During the missed week Daddy gives me the Narnia Chronicles. I read the first book. Then I read it to Eliza and Jim. The lion Aslan is so brave he's willing to be cut open for our sins. He gets tied up with ropes on a big stone table. When I read the stone table part Eliza and Jim start to cry. I don't tell them Aslan comes back to life. I tell them stay strong. Bear it. Then I point to the dark wardrobe in my room. I tell Eliza and Jim we'll push aside fur coats in the wardrobe then step into the ice of Narnia. We open the wardrobe. We step inside. We stand until the wardrobe crashes against my bed. Now we're trapped. We're going to die. We have to scream for our parents. Our parents pull the wardrobe up and push it against the wall. They ask us what the hell. Jim and Eliza look at my face. I can see they hate me. My eyes go blank with nothing. I'm not magic today.

In Andernos third grade doesn't matter. Our parents take us out of school before the year is done. Madame tells the class to write Au Revoir in big letters. I say goodbye to Pascal and my desk mate. Goodbye makes me sad even when I'm happy. I'm happy to drive around Europe with Mommy and Daddy and Jim and Eliza. We stay in campsites. Mommy and Daddy count the seconds while Eliza and Jim and I race to set up the blue tent. We get fast pushing the metal sticks into dirt. We tie the blue loops. We toss blankets from the tan car. We ask our parents did we beat the time? Three people sleep in the blue tent. Two people sleep in the tan car. At the campsites there are stand up bathrooms. You put your feet on footprints and pee in the hole between.

In the backseat of the car I make up friends for Eliza and Jim and me. I bend my fingers into shapes. There's Duck. Mad Duckter. Horse. Crocodile. Dog. Rabbit and Bent-Ear Rabbit. These friends live in a magic land where animals speak to kids but not grownups. Grownups are so gribouille they don't know the land can be reached by jumping into a gutter. You shut your eyes and when you touch the bottom of the gutter you swim through clear water until you get to Duckburg. In Duckburg the animals love you. My knuckles get sore when they talk. In my best story there is an evil committed by the Mad Duckter. He scares everyone so much they won't go to his castle. But Duck and Rabbit have grande valeur. They crash into the laboratory of the Mad Duckter and learn he's not evil. He is misunderstood. He has a brave heart but his Mad Duckter laugh gives the idea he's insane.

Our parents sit in the front seats with paper maps. There are pencil marks on famous cathedrals. To Eliza and Jim and me the cathedrals look the same. When the car stops we say "Oh no, another cathedral?" I look at the gargoyles. They stick out their tongues and their eyes bulge. One of them blinks. He is not evil. He is misunderstood. The gargoyle begs for help so I sneak him into the car. He crawls over the front seat. He grabs the steering wheel. He opens his wings of rock and knocks our parents unconscious. Eliza and Jim and I have to hitchhike by ourselves. In Paris we climb the Eiffel Tower with our bare hands. We go hand then hand then hand. That's the way through fear. You think about each bar and not the space between. Under my skin I am steel. I am made of metal knives that slice through dire doom. I am a surgeon. I cut the sky. I fly through the slit. Stitch it.

There's a closet behind the sky where everything goes blank. When Kimberly is a grownup I pull her in it sometimes. Her mind goes dark and empty and she doesn't feel she exists. I don't keep her always. I let her go if she's good.

Little One puts the pencil down.

"I'm tired. I want to be done." (Little One.)

Lola lifts her up. She and Wisp and Little One scatter away in the night, promising to return.

Chapter 13
Off Grid

In the morning Kimberly strings feathers from the casita ceiling. They flutter in a breeze as she sits at the kitchen table and sips a cup of coffee.

"I want to read your pages." (Kimberly.)

"They're not finished." (Me.)

"That's okay. I'll read what you have so far."

I give her the pencil words. Her forehead scrunches as she reads. Her eyes look sad, then fine, happy, fine, scared, fine, annoyed, fine, worried, fine, scared again, fine again, thoughtful finally, thinking hard, till she puts the pages down.

"I forgot about the rabbit." (Kimberly.) "I forgot about gribouilles."

"Is that all you have to say?"

"No. Give me a minute."

Kimberly pours more coffee. She steps outside the casita and breathes in juniper air. When she comes back her eyes are wet but she gives me a little smile.

"It's hard to read what you're writing. Sometimes I'm someone I recognize and sometimes I'm totally foreign. I know you're revealing myself to myself but again, and it's a question, is self a describable thing? And who am I without you all? Little One, Lola, Wisp and you?"

She sips her coffee, thinking more.

"And the question of memory, oh my god. How can we know what's true? Those memories of the van, Hollywood hills, a camera, they're so strange and extreme and yet we had them, didn't we."

"Yes."

"So

"Don't even ask me. Look at that doc in your laptop."

"I'm drinking coffee

"Do it. Whenever you go all fact-y and want to pin me down it helps to remind yourself. Do it. You'll feel better."

Kimberly opens her laptop.

"...Pierre Janet, who first explored the human response to trauma in detail, believed that vehement emotions interfere with people's capacity to cognitively integrate traumatic events. The terrifying nature of the event results in 'a phobia of memory' that prevents the integration and causes dissociation from ordinary consciousness. That is an excerpt from an article I read somewhere – maybe read more on Pierre Janet, 1919...? Also, 'The dialectic of trauma gives rise to complicated, sometimes uncanny alterations of consciousness, which George Orwell called 'doublethink'...' from an excerpt from Trauma and Recovery, Judith Herman, M.D…" *(Kimberly's laptop.)*

"There's more and more and more. You've read a million books on this. You know me. I have limits. Memory shifts its shape, plays with real/not real." (Me.)

"It's a gribouille."

"What?"

"Little One and her gribouilles. Memory starts as a dot of ink then bleeds to purple stain."

She looks at my worried face.

"It's okay. I'm okay. The truth is like watching clouds. There's a rabbit. There's a bird. There's a puffy lamb. If you point to a puffy lamb and your friend sees a rabbit instead, you're still both seeing the cloud." (Kimberly.)

The pages shake in her hand.

"And we were very young. Wow. We were young." (Kimberly.)

Kimberly puts down the pages. Her eyes look wet again as she grabs her jacket and bag.

"I need a break. Let's go." (Kimberly.)

To get to the big community pool Kimberly rides a bike. She takes a dirt path shortcut through a field of beat up houses. A yellow dog with huge sharp teeth stands up to bark and snarl. She stops her bike, startled. A man comes out of his door, shirt buttoned up all wrong. He smiles and waves her by. "He used to kill. Now he's old." She rides past the house as the dog limps off then lies down like ah fuck it. In the pool I rest while she strokes. There's a mountain out the window. Murals on the wall. We both relax in the water, losing thought as she swims.

In the open locker room shower, standing under the spray, Kimberly talks with two women. They haven't had a shower for what is it, honey, a week? Their voices are loud and throaty. They look high or maybe ill when they tell her Taos is amazing. It's full of people off the grid, that's what they are, off grid, and they laugh and shriek with each other as Kimberly dries with her towel. She puts on her thin black jeans and waves goodbye to them both. She pedals the bike real slow. When we're back inside the casita she looks at the wooden desk.

"Be careful with un-fearing." (Kimberly.) "Let's not lose our grid."

Chapter 14
Wisp

I am Wisp. I am year nine through ten.

My first order of business: Thank you Little One for writing up to Indiana.

My second order of business: I can't remember how we got back from France. I see the tan car hanging high from a rope as it swings onto a boat. That's all I can see. Maybe we ride a boat back to Les Etats Unis.

My third order of business: Indiana.

I do remember driving to Indiana. In the car I predict that Greencastle, Indiana will be a large castle covered in moss. It will be on a mountain like Mont-Saint-Michel. When the car stops I think darn it. Greencastle is a flat town. It is a white house on Hanna Street. It is woods and an accent called Hoosier. There are diagonal paths through a campus. The campus is smaller than UCLA but it has trees you can climb.

The best thing about Indiana is the marching band. The marching band marches by our house on Hanna Street. The leader of the band is a baton twirler named Candy. She is the first and most beautiful baton twirler I have ever seen. Eliza and I follow the band twirling sticks for batons. Candy and her band march by once a week. Other days there are pig trucks. We don't follow the pig trucks. You can smell them before they come and I've read Charlotte's Web.

In Indiana I start fourth grade. We use a pencil in school and I have to write slanted again. I continue to cross my number seven as I did in France but the teacher allows it. Our class is not doing fractions. We are starting multiplication. I finished multiplication in France so I start to get unpatriotic. I start to believe the school for dwarfs and serfs is ahead of this school. I sit behind a veneer of ennui. To break the veneer I look at rounded Ws on the black board and turn them into upside down birds. I decide Abraham Lincoln can be my best friend. Abraham Lincoln grew up nearby which is why I choose him. When I walk home from school Abraham and I discuss what has changed since he died. I explain what a car is. I introduce him to a telephone pole. I demonstrate the use of a gutter. He nods with interest.

On the classroom bulletin board is a density map. In Manitoba Canada there is only one person every ten square miles. I imagine living in Manitoba Canada with one person every ten miles and enjoy the idea.

Nellie Goodfellow lives in a tiny house behind our street. She crosses the grass to ask me if she may pick grapes from the grapevine in our yard. The previous renters let them. When I say yes she does a small curtsy. I am worried for her living with her grandmother alone in a one room house. I would like to know her but I don't see her in school.

At school in Indiana I touch my dress and knee socks. In this school I am rich. In this school Eliza is upset because she can no longer read. In Les Etats Unis an 'i' doesn't sound like 'eee.' Eliza sounds out the English words but they are no longer words. I tell her to be patient. She looks at me from her bed and throws her book at the wall. Eliza can be messy. I am not. I draw a line between our beds so my side can be neat. I worry about Eliza. I want her to read like she could in France because reading cures ennui.

I worry as well about Jim. When we walk to school Jim says he is disappearing. He lags behind and moves his legs in very slow motion. Jim's face is pale and his glasses tilt. I want to hug him always except when he won't walk. I say we are late for school. He says he has to move slowly. He shows me his wrist and arms. "Look. You can see my veins. I don't want to lose more weight." He is thin but sturdy. I suspect he is startled by the flat land and flat voices. I know I am. I shape my fingers into a duck and take us both to Duckberg.

On Easter we get a real duck. There is an Easter egg hunt on campus and the prize is a duckling whose name is BeerCan. Our parents are not pleased when we bring BeerCan home but they allow him to live in the bathtub. When he grows up he lives in a cage in the garage. He quacks very loudly when he follows us on the sidewalk. He quacks in the U-Shop where we buy gum for us and crackers for him. He is a white duck with orange feet. His feathers fly everywhere. His crap is a mess to clean up but I don't care about that. He is my favorite thing ever. The only element I don't enjoy is being in the garage. My father sometimes pins me there and does some things I dislike. Thankfully I forget them. I don't make clouds like Little One. I forget by making a compartment in my mind. I then take the compartment to the ledge of darkness where the girl stands tall and ready. She takes the compartment in her hands and crushes it to pearl. When Kimberly un-forgets I know the girl is Red Girl. I am very happy to meet her.

In Indiana my mother wants me to play the piano. Her sister played the piano in Nebraska and my mother enjoyed it. I learn to touch the keys. I master playing with one hand. When it comes time for me to play a song with both hands I am unable.

I get very frustrated and hide myself in a closet. Inside the closet I give myself a good talking to. I shake a finger at myself and use a mean voice to say "Don't be an idiot you can do this." When I leave the closet I am able to play the song with both hands. I decide you must get mean to yourself for results. I learn that the good talking to works for running and climbing high trees. It is also useful for holding your breath underwater and walking to school bare legged in below zero.

I use the good talking to at the football stadium. The football stadium is a short walk down Hanna street. I enjoy the football stadium because it has thin cement walls in front of the seats. I balance on the thin walls. I dare myself to leap over empty space and land on the other side. I never fall. This is because I do my good talking to every morning when I wake up. Sometimes I do my good talking to before I walk into the woods behind the stadium. I am not supposed to be in these woods but I enjoy them.

One day when I am in the woods I get scared. I am sitting on a moss rock near a creek. I notice I am alone. I am often alone but this time I notice. I have a strong feeling that no one knows where I am. I stare at the moss. I touch my braids. I tell myself if I had not had this notice thought I would not be scared. I stand up from the moss rock. I walk to

Hanna Street and open the door. My mother stands at the sink. I notice her not notice and I go back outside. I make a vow that I will stop all noticing.

I enjoy the tetherball pole at the playground of our school. At recess I hit the tetherball and watch it spin until it laces up the wooden pole. When it laces the pole and unwinds I hit it hard again. I become addicted. My parents give me my own tetherball so I can hook it on the wooden pole when school is closed. I take my tetherball to the playground even when the ground is covered with ice. I keep my vow of not noticing. I pretend I am in Manitoba Canada and I am one person every ten square miles. I hit my tetherball over and over and call it the head of a dead snowman. This is rather morbid. I know morbid means gruesome and grisly. Becoming morbid is why I prefer to be outside. I am much less morbid outside.

In the house I am prone to seeing invisible ghosts. I understand a person is not able to see something invisible. What I see is a ghost trace. A snail leaves a slime trace if you look closely. When I look closely at the inside of my house I see a ghost trace. I see a pale shadow that whips around corners when I walk down a hall. I see the same pale shadow in the steam over a pot of boiling potatoes. I see it in the dust of talcum. I see it in the pages of books.

In the house on Hanna Street bookshelves climb the walls. The bookshelves are full of poets and plays and novels. There is William Carlos Williams, Wallace Stevens, Charles Olson, Marianne Moore, Franz Kafka, Edward Albee and more than I can name. There is a shelf of books about religion and religious poetics and thick philosophy. These books are very important. Except when my father sneers and says what a pile of crap. Or no one needs a book. Or why does he bother with books. Or why are we trapped in this town. When my father looks out the window I hold the edge of a ghost. It chills my hand with cold dead air and carries me outside. The ghost will never tell me what my father wants. I know what he wants is not right here. Here is not enough.

I read a play from the bookshelf called "Who's Afraid of Virginia Woolf?" It is the first play I have ever read. As I read I see the blank spots between the talking. I understand that in the blank spots things happen. The things that happen are not explained so I read as hard as I can. I see that George and Martha live in a small college town like Greencastle. They yell and joke and drink. There is a secret between them about a baby. I begin to believe they have done something terrible with a baby. I believe they have killed it and buried it in their back yard. They lie to each other and pretend the baby is alive until George breaks the lie and calls it dead. Martha gets mad and cries.

I make a friend named Martha. She lives in a big house with two old people who look like grandparents. Their big house is full of tools and boards and furniture so close together we are unable to walk. There are chairs under tables and on top of tables. Martha's bed is upstairs in a room as full as a jammed closet. She says her parents are changing the house. They have been changing it since she was born. At school there are girls who make fun of Martha. I stick up for her when they do. I don't stick up for her because I am a nice person. I stick up for her because I know meanness will be directed at me if I don't. When I say "I like Martha" the girls look at me. I have moved from France. I am new and exotic. They change their minds and say "Okay. We like Martha too." I happen to know that when you are a new kid in school you are not in a group. You must show you don't care about a group. You must be your own girl.

I acquire another friend. Her name is Becky Little. This is ironic because she is not little. She is fat with red skin and shiny blond hair cut short like a helmet. She lives around the corner. In her yard are two bent lawn chairs. In one of the lawn chairs her enormous mother sits. Her mother's legs are mapped with blue veins that spread like the world over the shredded chair weave. Her dress is big. Her hair is strings. She is missing teeth. I am in awe. When I ask Susie where her father is she says "Oh. In jail." As if she were saying "Oh. At the U-shop." She asks me if I would like a stick of butter. I tell her I am not permitted to eat between meals. I am in awe again as she unwraps a stick of butter and eats it on the lawn. Her mother spreads over the chair looking at the street. I suspect she is waiting for the father to break out of jail and walk down the concrete.

I enjoy Hershel Shelton but he is not a friend. At recess he eats grasshoppers. Juice runs down his chin but he never dies from poison. One recess the teacher finds out he eats grasshoppers. She pulls a grasshopper out of his mouth while yelling "Hershel!" Then he has to stop. I enjoy Hershel because he has kind thoughtful eyes. I know he is not bright but I don't care. I think people with PhDs like Martha's husband George are unpleasant.

One afternoon I sell Girl Scout Cookies with my third friend Julie Halton. We walk door to door and while we walk a dirty red Volkswagen pulls up alongside us. We see a woman behind the wheel wearing red swimming goggles. She rolls down her window. Her face is painted white and her mouth is huge with lipstick. She tells us to get in her car. There's candy bars in front. Come on. Get in right now. She opens the door. She motions. We look and say no thanks.

She guns her motor and drives off. Julie and I sell a couple of cookie boxes. Then we knock on a door where no one is home. We hear a screech behind us. The goggle woman is back. She screams at us. "Get in the car! I will kill your parents!" Julie starts to cry. My feet move toward the car and I yell as loud as I can. "Shut up! Leave us alone!" I stare at her face. I clench my fists. I can hardly believe she goes. I run to my house still shaking. My parents make some calls. The campus police are aware. The woman showed up at a basketball game. She was maybe tripping. No one really knows.

Julie stays home for a week. She is too upset for school. I have to go to school. When I go I see the Volkswagen parked near Hanna Street. I see it every day. I point it out to Abraham. He nods with understanding. There is Party Weak and Party Strong. That's what my father tells me. The weak fall back. The strong go on. I am in Party Strong.

When summer comes I go with my Girl Scout troop to a production of Hansel and Gretel. It is the first play I have ever seen. I decide to write a play of my own. I make Eliza and Jim and Mary Cavenish who lives next door be in it. Writing the play and rehearsing and cutting the cardboard props takes an entire day. When the play is finished we perform it on the concrete slab of the driveway. For the rest of the summer I make up games.

My favorite game is Orphan. To play Orphan we become indignant that the Orphan Lady who runs the orphanage makes all the orphans work as slaves. Then we say to heck with it and sneak out of the orphanage. We race through the yard. There is an apple tree and a grapevine to keep us from starving. We jump for joy when we come to a small home. The home is a broken storage shed behind the Cavenish house. They do not mind at all if we clear it out and lie on the wooden shelves. At the shed cleaning part Eliza and Jim and Mary wander off and let me do it. They come back for the part where the Orphan Lady decides to come after us because she really and truly wants us despite her cold heart. That is when we eat chocolate cake made of leaves. Sometimes when I want to play Orphan Mary says no. She likes House. I tell her House is for babies. She tells me I am stuck up. She tells me her mother says so.

I watch my mother sew curtains and clothes. She makes a coat for my Barbie. She makes it with the same checkered cloth as her own coat. Some days I smash my Barbie's face and press her breasts with a pen. I twist her body into claws or bang her head on the floor. I know I should put on her coat. Instead I drag her by the ankles from Eliza's plastic horse named Comanche. Then I go to the railroad tracks to look for gold. Gold is plentiful near the railroad tracks. Every black rock carries a shiny vein or fish scale of yellow. I put the rocks in my pocket. I skip them at the river where I catch tadpoles. I hold tadpole jars to light. I watch specks of creek float like dust in a beam.

My mother has a big round stomach. When I look at her stomach I see ripples of small feet pressing like the feet of tadpoles. I start to dream of tadpoles growing feet. They crawl into the window of the bedroom I share with Eliza. They slither into my bed. There are Pampers and safety pins on a table. I will learn to pin Pampers on the new baby. I will love this. I will be a big help. The stomach looks big enough to burst. I worry my mother could die.

There is a library I walk to. I read open books of fairy tales and mysteries and histories of log cabins as I walk home. It is a summer of reading. Then something happens. I do my chores in the house. I put the dishes away. I push the chairs to the table and lie on the sofa to read. On the sofa I read about baseball to keep my mind off tadpole babies or dead mothers. My father walks into the room. He has been at the hospital. He says "Why are you lying there like a lazy princess? Your mother almost died and you're reading a book." I ask him what I am supposed to do. I always remember reading about baseball and asking my father what I am supposed to do. What I forget is being lifted from the sofa and taken into a room. I use my vow to not notice as I put the room into a compartment. The room does not contain my father's desk and a crib for the new baby. The room does not have bamboo blinds on the windows. My father does not shove himself in me while my mind screams Is Mommy Dead Is Mommy Dead. My father does not tie my hands to a doorknob. My father does not hurt me. My father does not laugh when he unties me. I do not type I hate I hate I hate on his typewriter. I do not promise I will write him dead someday. I do not cry.

My mother brings home a baby named Colin. I learn to hold his head. I learn to wipe his bottom. I watch the tadpole of his belly button turn into a small twig. I flick it from my finger into an open Pamper. I am a perfect helper but one day I make a mistake. Colin has learned to crawl and I forget I am watching him. I don't know why I forget. When my parents come home they see him on the sidewalk. You should hear the yelling. My parents tell me I am grounded for the rest of my life. I become so enraged I forget about Becky Little's birthday party. When I tell Becky I am sorry I forgot her birthday party she says nothing.

On the plus side of my existence I am in the same school. Fifth grade is the first time I have gone to the same school. I fall in love. There is a boy in my fifth-grade class I do not know at all. He has blue eyes and torn jeans. One day my fifth-grade teacher Mr. Avery tells Shane to lift up his shirt. This is to show us why he was out of school last week. There are tubes coming out of Shane. The waste from his body will move through the tubes and land in hanging bags. I want to touch the tubes. I want to touch his skin. Shane puts his shirt down. His face goes red as he sits. I cannot remember if he spoke or if he stayed in school. I wish I could have known him. I really really loved him and my love is big and true.

In fifth grade there are bombs that will fall any minute smack dab on Indiana. We are told to go under our desks. We are told to put our hands on the back of our neck. I do not believe my hands will stop a bomb and I do not believe anyone else believes. I become morbid thinking of adults doing pretend things like calling a school desk a bunker. When I become very morbid I go to the back yard and climb my tree. A branch is a hard chair but it is better than the sofa. I read my books on the branch. One afternoon on the branch I hear my parents. They mention a bigger college and leaving this flat little town. My mother's voice is happy. I put my hands on my knees and crunch so they won't see me. I think goodbye to Abraham. I think goodbye to Martha. I think goodbye to Shane. I don't think goodbye to BeerCan. Weeks ago he left his cage.

Eliza and Jim and I ran up and down the sidewalks calling out his name. Someone told us he was seen in the aisles of the U-Shop pecking at crackers.

Before we leave Indiana I see a white duck in the lake of a state park. I say to my mother "There's BeerCan safe in the wild." My mother asks how I know it is BeerCan. "Because he has a bent neck. BeerCan's neck got bent when that man pulled him out of the kiddie pool screaming I will kill this thing if you don't keep it in your yard." My mother says "Oh yes. It must be BeerCan." I am aware she is humoring me.

Goodbye goodbye goodbye. See ya down the pike. All's well that ends well. Hail good fellow well met. Sayonara baby. These are the words in my mind as we drive from Indiana. When Kimberly is an adult I use them to help her go on. I tell her chin up. Keep going. Never ever notice a thing you love and lose.

Wisp twirls the pencil.

"I could write more but I shan't."

We roll our eyes at shan't. Wisp takes Little One by the hand and laughs as she swings her up.

Chapter 15
Ants

I put the pages of Wisp on the table in the casita. Kimberly reads with a scrunched up face. Then she wants a walk.

We take her favorite path. A short hill, turn to the left, then a red dirt road. You come to a fence that's always shut but you can walk around. Then you see the morada. The morada's a cracked adobe house with a door that's painted blue. Stretching from the morada is a long and rutted path that leads to a wooden cross. Kimberly stands on the rutted path. Silks of purple blanket the sky. Balls of brush are fists. All is clear shimmer.

The morada and cross and path belong to the Penitentes. Penitentes kneel in dirt and beat themselves with sticks. They walk on their knees down the rutted path with the wooden cross on their backs. It's an old ecstatic worship, an entry to the divine, that centuries back was outlawed by Spain but here, in northern New Mexico, still goes on in secret. Kimberly walks the rutted path then finally speaks to me.

"What if writing invisible heart is self-flagellation and torture. What if we're dragging

ourselves through dirt as a masochistic act."
(Kimberly.)

I don't know what to say. I mention morbid. We make it a noun. Morbidiosity. Then Kimberly sits in the dirt and draws a ? with her finger.

"When I picture you in my brain, you and Little One, Lola and Wisp, I see a plastic ant farm. Jim had one, remember? I see you all as ants, burrowing through my tunnels and carrying stuff away."

"Well ants work hard."

"Yeah. But forgetting so much of my life is kind of stressing me out. Wisp and that room I forgot. How did I forget that? I don't understand, well yeah, I do, but today, after reading her words, it seems completely bizarre. I know the moving didn't help, all the constant change. How can you make a story, a story to be trusted, that tells you who you are. You know? You know what I'm saying?"

"You're wishing you had some roots."

Kimberly's eyes go far away and I see that I was right. Her two least favorite questions are where did you grow up and are your parents alive. I'm not from a place and I think they're alive sound like feeble answers, always and more so today, sitting by the morada, watching ants in the dirt. She knows she's not unique, plenty of people are rootless, but there are times, now is one, when the weight sits like a rock. She moves an ant with a finger and heaves herself up with a shake.

"Let's go. I'm ready to go." (Kimberly.)

Back at the casita, Lola shows up alone.

Chapter 16
Lola

I'm old as the fucking hills and soft as a rotten peach but I'll start in year eleven.

I'm on a school bus with new morons. What does Delaware? Her New Jersey. My parents have dragged us to Delaware. Kill me now and la-di-da. Delaware's the first state. The state bird is a small ass blue hen whose head looks as brainless as my seatmate's. There's no forest near Putrid Lane. No Candy and marching band. There's curbs and rectangle yards and sorry ass naked sidewalks. The houses all look the same. Triangle over the door. Cut short lawn in front.

The kid sitting next to me gets off on torturing cats. He put one near the school bus wheel then laughed when it almost died. His friends all yukked it up too. I look out the window at nothing while they yell at the school bus driver. The driver will quit next week. We'll get a few more drivers until every kid on our route is called to a special assembly. Shape up or else, you kids. Sure and hahaha.

I write some letters to Martha. I write that I hate Delaware so much I can't breathe. I live in a gray fog.

I miss BeerCan and Abraham Lincoln and my life as a Girl Scout. I even miss the pig trucks. I carve out helpless words like I'm throwing them in a bottle. This is my first gray fog. It could be hormones, sure. It could also be the lawns. Every single one reeks of pathetic sameness. I wander and look for woods but I'm stuck with a 7-Eleven. Even that's a hike. When I get there, big so what. I'm too broke for a Slushie.

I thank my nonexistent tits for a man named Mr. Noble. He's the gym teacher for sixth grade. He really is noble. An hour before school starts he opens the gym for any desperate twit who wants to do gymnastics. Call me one of those twits. For an hour before school and for an hour after I leap and do cartwheels and flips. Eliza does this too. We have a bike to share, so instead of riding the school bus I stand up and pedal while she's on the seat. Sometimes we switch it around. We pedal to school every morning then twist our bodies like screws. We backbend into circles and flip ourselves through air and it throws the gray fog from my body. I stop missing Indiana. It fades like a streak of bleach.

I survive sixth grade and seventh grade. In eighth grade I suck up the courage to ask Mom for a bra. She tells me I don't need one. I know my chest is flat as a damn ironing board but the other girls have bras. I say this to Mom in the kitchen and she lets out a big ass sigh. A few weeks later she hands me a training bra. It gets snapped by the cat killers. Every day at school there are hands on my back. I want to punch the fuckers but instead I stare ahead.

In the yard next door is a baton twirler. She's younger than Candy but older than me. She throws the baton in spirals and I never see her miss. Sometimes she sets it on fire. I watch her from my yard but we don't ever talk. She twirls and throws and concentrates and I want to be that perfect. I'm not perfect at all. My underarms sweat in wet triangles. My hair greases. I have thin down on my legs. I worry about pubic hair. I worry about everything. Finally I get a boyfriend. We kiss against walls. We lick with tongues. We declare love for all time and throw ourselves on grass. On Putrid Lane kids want games of keep away or rough tag that leave us piled in heaps. We breathe each other's sweat. We scratch and bite and bruise. It's boys on girls and girls on boys and the smell of mud and lawn. We know it's now or never. We're on the cusp of almost grown so enjoy it while we can.

After school I'm clearing the table and hear my dad say my friends are stupid. I put the dishes down. I get pissed off and leave. I might even slam the door. When I'm on the sidewalk I look around and see my zero options. I head to the creek behind the school where there's a big ass tree. A rope hangs down from a branch to swing you over the water.

Ages ago some high school kids dared me to climb up the tree then crawl out onto the branch and touch where the rope is tied. The branch is high and narrow and they smoked while they watched me touch it. After I touch it once I start to climb alone. I tell Mom I do this and she says I'll be okay. Even if I fell, at worst I'd break an arm. I feel a kind of comfort. Then I go big duh. She's never seen the tree. I could break my neck.

I sit on the branch and think. I know my friends are stupid. We're stuck on concrete curbs. Mom says get yourself out there, time to make new friends, and when I do, oh fuck it. I hurl her into the creek. She swims like a drowning Barbie and I feel a kind of glee. I tie my dad from the rope. Die why don't you, die. But the rope hangs empty as a noose and Mom isn't really drowning. I stare at the creek below. I consider jumping. I don't, of course, big duh, I mean I'm here to write this, but I do throw parts of myself. I toss off Little One's magic. I throw down Wisp's no notice. I watch them swirl in the muddy creek as I bite the hump of my tongue. I'm old now. Nothing works. I can't believe in magic. Good talking to does nothing. I grip the branch and stare. Who am I. What can I be. Then it comes. Big idea. I'll work my butt off every day and strive to succeed in school. Striving will make a thick wall between me and myself. I'll hide behind the wall and live on the other side. I'll push myself to a future. I'll ram myself ahead. I'll run so fast and strive so hard I'll never be where I am.

My planning gets interrupted by the sound of my boyfriend's voice. I love my boyfriend's voice but now it sounds like clay. Thick and kind of mumbly and a little bit worried and pointless. My boyfriend has bad ass hair that reaches to his shoulders. Some lady who saw us on our bikes thought he was a girl. That's only because of his hair. He's skinny and tough and has this air that gets me to ask for advice. I like to pretend he's older but really we're both thirteen. When I climb from the branch to be with him I'm surprised to feel the wall. I didn't think it would start so soon but who am I to stop it. My boyfriend saw my parents. They think I'm running away for good so they asked him to try and find me. We sit together by the creek and throw some sticks in the water.

My boyfriend's dad told him last week that he's a loser who should be more like me. His dad has met me exactly once. I could be a shoplifter like our friend Tina who steals dime store earrings to see what happens. I tell my boyfriend I have to stop seeing Tina because stealing is not striving and it will break the wall I plan to work on. I don't think he hears me. His voice keeps mumbling like clay and his face looks kind of worried. I worry about him looking worried then worry about myself. The tree I climbed starts to seem like a mirage. I'm beginning to know that when things go into mirage it means I'm scared. I can know when I'm scared but not what I'm scared of. I ask my boyfriend if he ever gets scared for no reason. He says everyone's scared of shit, it's normal and so am I. I throw my last stick in the water, glad he said I'm normal. I don't believe he knows but I pretend he does. I promise to walk back home and we make out in goodbye.

In the house Dad hugs me in the living room. He didn't mean what he said. My friends aren't stupid and neither am I. I'm bright and really special. I'm wonderful. I'm loved. Please don't run away. Please don't do that again. A guilt swims in my body. It flips through my blood like a fish and I know this fish. It's always there. It swims and courses through me like it owns my sorry ass. I'm a pond of scum and the fish survives on me. Guilty as charged. Guilty. Guilty guilty guilty for wanting to hate my parents. For tying my dad to a rope and throwing my mom in the creek. For wanting to run away. For trying to get the hell out. My dad doesn't mean to be mean. When his own dad died he was sent to boarding school at thirteen. He lived in boarding school until Princeton, Air Force, us, and when you live in institutions, only institutions, it can fuck you up. I understand, I understand, and I promise to never leave. I go into hiding, deep behind the wall.

I work on getting A's. I laugh at every joke. I'm light as a goddamn creampuff and exhausted every day. I run ahead of my guilty fish with apology in my ears. Sorry to be here. Sorry to be. Sorry to bother you all. The apology tune becomes a loop, this endless bang in my head, and it's there all the fucking time. I start to go a bit cracked but no one seems to see. Eighth grade halls are crowded and lots of kids are a mess. I'm not special, not at all, no matter what my dad says. I could have lost my shit that year if he hadn't bought the cabin.

The cabin is deep in nowhere next to a lake in Maine. Ten miles down a dirt road is the nearest small ass town. You might think I'd hate spending a summer in a two room cabin with my parents and Eliza and Jim and Colin and Susie and no electricity or neighbors or town but I don't. I've never heard such silence. I've never felt the blackness of a night with no light. I listen to loons. I listen to water lapping. Sometimes I listen to the grinding sound of the generator we use twice a week for hot water. For drinking we fill cups from a spring flowing through a plastic tube. At night we light Coleman Lanterns.

The lake is alive in different ways. Somedays are calm. Somedays are wild. Somedays are choppy and dark. We swim in it every day and it becomes my skin. At night I dream of mermaids who carry me like a coffin on top of their skinny shoulders. I'm peaceful as a queen and school is far away.

In the center of the lake are two white rocks. Eliza and Jim and I decide we have to get there. We work on our strength by running obstacle courses. Touch the stump, run to the tree, ten pushups then jump over logs. We time ourselves and we beat our times but still the rocks are far. Two little specks in the big ass blue and we don't want to drown. Then a miracle comes. We're resting on the dock that floats in front of the cabin when a broken rowboat passes. It's floating by like a damn mirage so we pull it out of the water and turn it upside down. We cut long pieces of string and shove the string in the floor cracks. We chop thin logs for oars. We search underneath the cabin to find two pieces of wood. We paint the pieces brown then nail them onto the logs. The oars look like big fudgesicles but we swear to god they'll work.

We slide our boat in the lake. Water spouts in through the cracks so we find a tin can to bring. We row and bail and row and bail. We watch the cabin get smaller. We search for the dock that floats but we can't even see it. If we were standing on the dock we'd play rock paper scissors. The rules are one-two-three rock paper scissors go. If you lose you move to the next wooden board on the dock. Then the next board, then the next, until you have to jump off the dock or get pushed. We yell when we hit the water. We see fish in green fog. When we catch these fish we flip them back after pulling hooks from their mouths. In the boat we talk about fishing. That time when Jim caught an eel. We screeched like wild geese and I ran to the cabin kitchen. With a potholder mitt I held the eel, oh my god, oh my god, the way it twisted up, wrapping itself around my arm, and who finally pulled the hook? Was it Jim? Eliza? Both? We threw the eel in the air, it curled and flicked away, and it could be swimming now, it could be right under. We drag a hand in the water to swirl the surface and look. Insects flicker and skate. Our tin can shines with slime. We raise our eyes to the shore. The cabin is out of sight but sound still travels the lake. We can hear Colin dimly. He was too young to come.

I feel a sudden love that circles like a ring. It grows and grows and grows till I can barely stand it. There's nothing between myself and me and the wall has fallen down. The apology tune is gone, lifted into air. I'm brother. Sister. Water. Ripples calm and lapping. The circles expand and hover as I shove an oar in the lake. We row and bail and row and bail till we bump against the rock. Oh look, it's not two rocks. It's one with jutting points. Oh wow, the white is bird shit. We scramble onto the rock. We dangle our feet in the water and hold the boat with the rope. What if we let it go? We'd have to live here forever, marooned on a bird shit rock. Unless someone saw us. But who. Boats are rare on the lake. If we see a boat from the cabin deck we point and call to each other. Could we survive on fish? We think, feet in the water, then think about thinking itself. What's the point of thinking. Why did thoughts evolve. There's a man with a big house on the dirt road who teaches philosophy in Boston. A few times he and Dad have discussed theories of mind and consciousness and other things we strive to understand. When we consider the evolutionary purpose of thinking we come up short. Do birds have consciousness. And what's it called when you think about thinking.

Jim smacks a fly. I see the welt on his shoulder forever and today. No more of this talk, we're done. He steps in the boat. I hold the rope. Eliza gets in. Then me. I push my foot on the rock and give the boat a shove. Jim rows. Eliza bails. I watch the ripples circling and want the sudden love. Brother. Sister. Water. Ripples calm and lapping. It's now become elusive, a slippery thing that leaves, so back at the cabin, on the deck, I squint my eyes at the lake. I see a blur and ripple and feel myself in light. I look at my family shining. Colin plays with a truck. Jim spools his fish line. Eliza sits on the railing in a saddle made from a towel. Ropes hang down for stirrups, a clothesline's held for reins, and she trots or gallops through her fields, a stick in her hand, riding far, all the way to her edges. My parents point to Susie. She's lapping water from the spring. I want to hold the feeling, catch it in a glass. I want to write it down.

I walk to the blue tent behind the cabin. It's the same blue tent that travelled all over Europe in the trunk of the car. The tent's now saggy under trees, covered in bugs and mosquitos. I open the flap and crawl inside then zip the triangle tight. I want to write the flicker, the feeling on the lake. Brother. Sister. Water. Ripples calm and lapping. I don't know what to call it. I choose "elusive love." Pitiful words but all I have and I will make them do. I look at the typewriter on a stool. It's a black manual Dad is using to write an academic book about a poet and also, I see, some short stabs at fiction. His narrator's opening sentence describes a fictional family dying in a plane crash. I know I'm spying and doing wrong, but I look at the pages and read the words and they pull me in, drug like, to the world of my dad, the world of me, mysteries deep and gripping. There's a smell of sweat in the tent. It's cloth and bracken and pine and my eyes swim out and up. I feel the hole inside myself, the missing piece, the longing, the empty space where I lose my shit and hate myself for something. The typewriter stares at my face. I want to smash it in half, with no idea why I do. I put his pages down and sit on the floor of the tent. I can't write elusive love. It's gone, the feeling's gone, and there's something I don't want to know. Something I have to hide. I crush a mosquito in my hand, wondering what the hell. I don't know what I'm hiding, I don't know what it is, but after Kimberly un-forgets I know what I used to do. I do it now in the tent. I smear my thoughts with Vaseline to cover all the shit. Every bad thing that happens goes hazy and streaky and slick, an oily mess of mirage, and I smear and smear and smear until I slide away. I slide away from deep in the woods, running as fast as I can, thrown on the ground, done to, then tossed in the lake with a laugh. I slide away from a fishhook pushed inside my body. I slide away from the pillow, Mom holding it on my face, as Dad swears up and down I pushed it in myself. I slide away from the window, Mom driving the car without me, as I bang on the glass and beg to get in, don't leave me here alone. I slide away from years and years of impossible things to know. Now inside the blue tent, not knowing yet, not knowing, I feel the guilty fish swim up, rising and making me sick. I'm no innocent girl. I'm a worm on the end of a hook. How dare I write elusive love when I have to break up with my boyfriend.

The letter I write him is short. I write that we're in a beginning. The first year of high school is in the fall so I want to be pure and new. I don't know what this means or why the hell I write it. I can barely remember Putrid Lane. School. The creek. His face. This summer I've climbed big hills. I've fished and rowed and bailed and found some bones on a rock. I've walked for miles on long dirt roads, crushed blueberries in my fist. I'm no longer the girl he knew. I'm a girl who has to break up. I sign the letter and fold it and zip up the tent when I leave.

On a drive to town for the laundromat I ask to stop at the post office. I stamp my letter and mail it. Driving back to the cabin I remember my boyfriend's face. I watch my own face bob in the reflection of the window. I put my fingers on my lips to curl them in a smile. That night I scream in my sleep. I don't know I'm screaming. I hear my parents wake me up to tell me that I am. In the morning, on the deck, I say I dreamed of a pointy fish that chased me up a tree. It chomped my feet as I climbed, so on top of the tree I turned around and screamed out "let me go!" My family laughs and shakes their heads. They love to hear my nightmares. They ask me to tell another one but I pick at a huge mosquito bite and say they'll have to wait. Then I laugh, the way they laugh, and look out over the lake.

When summer ends it's back to school. Back to school is suckwad. The apology tune starts up and my wall gets really thick. I strive to get those A's but every day throughout ninth grade I wonder when we'll move. Before gymnastics and after school I swing on the short trapeze that hangs from a tree in our yard. I made the trapeze in seventh grade to have a place to think. In the summer before I made it we lived in London then Switzerland. In London Dad did research at the British Museum. I have no idea what he did in Switzerland. Eliza and Jim and I were sent to an alpine camp. Cows wore clanging bells and I slept by myself in a room. There were shutters on the window with a mademoiselle who closed them, "Nous fermons pour la nuit," until finally one night I asked, in broken French, I've forgotten my French, if we could leave them "ouvre." She smiled and said "Mais oui." Word created action! I'm in that moment a verb! I was too pleased, I know that now, by a simple request that was simply heard but at the time it was golden. So were the trapeze girls. They performed near the alpine camp and I studied their every move. They gripped the ropes, bent their backs, held themselves at angles, and on Putrid Lane, remembering this, I hang upside down by my ankles. My parents like to move. I know we're going to move.

The new house they get is old. I scrape layers of wallpaper and the balls of gray stick on my arms and legs. Under the curling trees are plaids, then dots, then squares, then any color I want. I streak my walls with yellow paint and make my door go purple. On this new street the houses are not the same. Some are wood, some are stone, and my window looks on a yard. At least it's in the same town. I'd bolt if I had to change school.

I quit gymnastics. For years I've spent every school night and every Saturday at a training center going nowhere. Eliza is good. I'm not. I do like hurling myself in the air but sometimes I throw up. I decide it's time for a change, some kind of needed change, but I'm whacked by the change when it comes. I grow a brand new body. Breasts. Hips. Holy shit. That's what they say at school. I get called beautiful but don't believe it. I stand in front of the mirror to stare at myself each day. I see pimples on pale skin. Wavy hair when straight is better. Skinny scabbed up legs holding a curved and foreign thing. I see a statue in the mirror that stares with stranger eyes. That's when I'm in mirage land so I have to go next door.

Next door is Nancy. On Nancy's front door is a string of bells. Her parents tell me not to ring the bells, just walk into the house. I can never walk into the house. I stand outside the door, waiting, trying, waiting, until Nancy finally sees me. When I walk inside with Nancy there's food and classical music. Nancy's stepmother has a large loom in the middle of the house and she weaves to music. She also serves food from a store in New York City called Zabars. On the table she puts out liverwurst and pickles and rounds of weird cheese. At my house meals are waited for and I snack on dry spaghetti. At Nancy's I stuff my face. After I stuff my face we usually go to her room. Nancy smokes cigarettes while she reads books like "War and Peace." She gets perfect grades and perfect SAT scores but I never see her study. We're friends because she lives next door and we take the same acting class at school. On the first day of the acting class the teacher says "lie on the floor and pretend you're on a beach." Then she says "notice what you're feeling." I've never been asked in all my life to notice what I'm feeling. I notice I live in a shell and don't ever want to come out. I notice that when I do come out I'm supposed to be someone else. Acting is all pretend and I love being someone else.

Nancy and I learn the sign language alphabet for a play we perform for deaf kids. At school we lower our hands at our desks and use our fingers to spell deep secrets like "This class is boring" or "Gavin's fucking cute." After school we walk to the wall on Main Street. We sit on the wall to look at college guys and smoke Kools. Nancy has a brother in medical school. She wants to be a doctor but says her family won't pay for it. We say unfair and exhale.

It sucks to be a girl. Not because you're a girl. I say it's because there's a girlness that exists like a mirage. In the mirage I can't talk back. I can't make an egg if I haven't made one for my brother first. I wonder how my mom can read books like "The Second Sex" and "Feminine Mystique" and still believe the mirage. She works sometimes as a teacher. She also does the laundry, the hanging of laundry in the basement, the cleaning of the whole house, the cooking of all meals, the sewing of all clothes, the packing for all moves. It seems to me that a real Feminine Mystique would not do these things without screaming. My mom never screams. All she does is sigh or lie on the living room sofa curled up in a ball. Sometimes when she does this I take over. Other times I say fuck it and wait the whole spell out. Nancy says it does seem to be the agreement that things involving kids or houses or touching of uncooked food or cleaning of unwashed items is best done by Second Sex hands. Maybe that will change someday. We say yeah right and inhale.

Nancy can't stop the apology tune that bangs around in my head. What stops that tune is sex. I get a new boyfriend old enough to buy beer. He has his own apartment so sometimes I ride my bike to school instead of taking the school bus. I stop by his place in the morning and we do it until homeroom. Sex is how I'm real. I dive inside my body and it blows away the mirage. Except I never come. I can when I'm by myself but with him it doesn't happen. When I tell Nancy this she looks at me with pity. Maybe that will change someday. We say yeah right and laugh.

Dad doesn't like this boyfriend. Big so what. He hates them all. I don't fully know this yet but after France I do. In the summer before twelfth grade I get to go to France. I worked my butt off to finish high school in three years so our family could go some place for Dad's sabbatical year. The some place doesn't happen. I've forgotten why. Maybe I never knew. I do know I get to go to France as reward for working my butt off. I'm going on a six-week summer language program by myself until I find out Dad wants to go too. I have no say at all in this as I'm never a goddamn verb. We take the plane together while Mom and Colin and Jim and Eliza and the new dog Luke stay in Delaware.

In France I spend six weeks blasting the apology tune out of my body. I flirt, smoke, espresso drink and learn some ways to come. The program has a music school so I go for a horn player, a classical guitar player, and a flutist. I'm mais oui mais oui and do you parler that? I watch myself for six whole weeks the way I'd watch a movie. I'm a driven need and love's not a thing elusive, love is slamming here, love is in their eyes. When I'm not doing mais oui I read big books in French. I read while I sip wine and think about my future. I don't see my boyfriend in it. There's something about a boyfriend that makes me feel tied up. I'd rather be alone.

I write him a break up letter. He writes back that he's bummed. I write back that I'm sorry. He writes back that he gets it. All is well until the day of the flight home with my dad. For unknown reasons my dad went into my room and read my mail. I'm not there when he does this. I find out at the airport. He looks like someone I've never met as his eyes go cold and hard. He tells me he wants to shoot my boyfriend. My dad is a liberal pacifist with no gun so I know he won't really do this. What scares me is the way he glares at me and says I'm in trouble big time just wait till we get home. I hide in the airport bathroom, staring from the toilet. I go into deep mirage where everything seems not real except I know it is. I stay on the toilet so long I almost miss the plane.

At home Mom calls me a slut. She tells me to live with my boyfriend and never come back. I leave the house in the dark and sit my ass on a curb. I think about existence and what the hell I am. There's kids who run away. They get dragged back or disappear and I'm not stupid, am I. I've got my job at Burger King but there's no car, no place to live. Maybe next door with Nancy. No, that thought is suckwad. If I lived next door with Nancy my parents would see me there. And I want to go to college. I need my parents for that. At least I think I do.

I scratch the skin of my ankles. I scratch it to bloody grooves. I tell myself to suck it up, tell them all I'm sorry. I stand up from the curb then walk through the dark and the streetlights and enter the house real quiet. Mom is in the basement, glass of wine in her hand. She tells me I'm like her sister. Stubborn. Foolish. Wild. I tell her I've nowhere to go. She looks at me in a silence. I sit on the basement steps. We stay like that for hours, or maybe the rest of our lives. The silence has a pulse. It beats like a little drum. Da-dum, da-dum, I'm sorry. Da-dum, da-dum, you should be. It beats and beats between us familiar as my skin.

Lola stops the pencil and shimmers across the desk.

"I hate the way I sound! I'm like this crawling pleaser that fucked up Kimberly's life. I made her do all kinds of things she didn't want to do." (Lola.)

"That's not your fault."

"Whose is it? I could have walked in the house and told them all the truth."

"You didn't know the truth

"I should have known

"You couldn't

"I shouldn't have smeared all the shit. I shouldn't have slid away. I shouldn't have dumped it all on you to hold on your dumbass ledge. I should have been stronger. Better."

Lola looks like a broken thing as she tries to keep from crying. When she burst out of invisible heart she thrilled me with her force. Now she breathes in shaky breaths that barely let her speak.

"I blocked it out for him. Not for me, for him. Can you forgive that?" (Lola.)

"There's nothing to forgive."

"But I couldn't care for us. I protected him."

"Lola

"I know what I did. Don't say it's not my fault."

She shows her face for a moment. She's streaked with shame and mascara and she leaves me in a flash.

Now, at the casita desk, I smell cheap musk and gin. I touch the pencil to my cheek. I write "I love you Lola."

Chapter 17
Charred Wood

Kimberly reads the words. Her face is quiet and still as she laces up her boots.

We hike a trail that's steep and high and winds us back and forth. At the very highest point is a low throne made of rocks. Kimberly sits on the throne. She looks at the campfire circle that's huge and ringed with soot. The circle's full of old charred wood that sends up a smell of smoke. Our minds stretch out and ramble as we sit in open silence.

"Thank you for writing, Red Girl." (Kimberly breaking the silence.)

"It's hard and I get tired."

Kimberly steps from the throne. She kneels in the circle of campfire and picks up a piece of charred wood. She holds the wood in her hand, looking much too thoughtful.

"But you'll keep going, yeah?"

I look at her unsure. Kimberly drops the wood from her hand and steps herself out of the circle. She lifts her face to the sun as a hawk goes floating by. She puts her finger to her lips, agreeing to my silence. No more words, not today, nothing more between us.

Chapter 18
Change

I need the Laughing Corpse so I jump to the dungeon mind. I'm surprised by change. Little One's closet door swings open on its hinges. There's a new book under Wisp's old tree and Lola's cigs, smoked to the butts, are neatly stacked in rows. I shuffle through piles of pages to reach the girl-at-her-desk. Her chair is empty and cold. The golden squirrel still stands on his pin but I notice, touching him now, that his missing eye is back. I kiss the brand new ruby then see the report I left.

Favorite Part: _Elusive love._

Least Favorite Part: _Lonely._

I yell for the Laughing Corpse. When he presses my shoulders lightly I jump from the desk and grab him. My feelings bubble out, spilling into his chest.

"I should have said no to the bear. I should have grabbed his porridge. I should have kept Kimberly out of here

"It's alright, it's alright

"Every word I write is a cut inside my heart!"

"Calm down, Red Girl

"No. It's like my skin is gone, peeled away and hot, and my heart goes scared and thumpy

163

whenever I touch the pencil. Tell me I'm safe, tell me I'm good, tell me that what I'm writing won't mean death by drowning, tell me

"Is Kimberly kind?"

"Only because of this."

I lift up my hair to show the bone. It's gone. It's no longer there. My fingers touch my scalp, racing through my tangles.

"Where is it? Where is it?" (Me.)

The Laughing Corpse steps away to look for it on the ground.

"You're limping." (Me.)

"Yes. I took a fall on a stone. Some are coming loose."

"What's going on here?"

"Think."

The Laughing Corpse turns to face me. I see in his eyes the answer.

"I'm changing us, aren't I."

He nods. I sit myself in the empty chair and feel a surge of fear. I pick up the golden squirrel. My writing is changing the dungeon mind and I don't want it to change.

"If I finish writing invisible heart, will you fly with me?" (Me.)

"Yes."

"Is that a promise?"

"Yes. I'll be with you forever Red Girl."

I sit in his lap of bones and he breaks off another finger. I shake my head, not needing.

"Your promise is enough."

Chapter 19
Fear of Change

When I jump back from the dungeon mind Kimberly's in the kitchen. She puts the pages down and looks at me over her coffee.

"I didn't know you were scared of change." (Kimberly.)

"Yeah, well I didn't either."

"Don't stop writing, please."

"Did you say please?"

"Oh."

Kimberly's face goes red. She doesn't like to need me, so she pours more coffee into her cup as if I'm barely there. I put on my bravest face and let the pencil move.

Year twenty-eight. Manhattan.

Kimberly's on a bed. She lies on her side, crying. Her fiancé, raised in Manhattan, a man who believes in therapy, wipes her smudged mascara and suggests she might, maybe, perhaps, consider a bit of help.

The therapist is a solid gray-haired woman who sits on a cushioned chair. Kimberly tells her she's happy. The happiest she's ever been. In love.

Engaged. A stepmom. Still, and this is a problem,
she cries every day like a clock. The therapist nods
her head. Kimberly speaks in a rush. She's always
felt she's running, trying to run away. She went to
college out of state. B.A. English Lit. Survival jobs
through college. Pizza maker. Office work. Library
filing, yakety yak, then on to acting school. Acting is
what she likes. She moved to New York after acting
school but still, and this is a problem, cried every
night in her sleep. She doesn't know what she's
running from. Life is good, life is fine, but she carries
a grip inside her, she feels a kind of grip, that sits in
her body, heavy, pulling her into a well. She runs
ahead of the grip. If she stops for a moment, ever
stops, the grip takes hold, grabs her, pulls her and
won't let go, so she runs to stay in front, running
with action and thought and busy busy busy to
cover the noise, the noise of the grip, and as
Kimberly yaks and yaks I see the grip is me.

I don't want her yakking. I don't want this room.
I scrunch myself in invisible heart and hold my
breath real tight. If Kimberly hears me breathe we
won't have a family, we won't have a life, we'll be
stinky shitty crap that reeks of the old dead sock. I
stay inside the invisible heart, squeezing hard,
holding my breath, while Kimberly yaks away. Her
life's a breezy breeze, so what the hell and what. No,
she has no eating disorders. She does like to smoke.

She does on occasion drink too much. No, she's never felt she belongs anywhere. But with the exception of frequent moves she sees no reason, none at all, for the piercing pulling grip that chases her like a wind.

I don't stop holding my breath. I hold it hold it hold it while Kimberly yaks in the room. Once a week for a month. Two months. Six months. Twelve months. A year. Another. Another. Four whole years of pointless water torture. Drip drip drip, "parentified," plink plink plink, "no roots," drip drip drip "no self-worth," plink plink plink, "try meds," drip drip drip "they didn't work," plink plink plink, "well, now let's try" till I'm suffocating and damp and ready to shout "Shut up!"

There's Party Weak and Party Strong and Party Weak is whiners. I'm in Party Strong. I stand up tall, dance on the ledge, die for the good of all. I'm saving Kimberly, that's my job, why won't she let me do it? Why won't she shut up? I hold and hold and hold my breath (Party Strong Party Strong) while she yaks about her dreams. When she's asleep I'm Party Weak. I lose my grip on invisible heart and dreams slip out like fish. Dreams like deaf people can't hear you scream. Or you're buried alive. Or you crawl through caves to escape concentration camps. Or guards chase you and threaten to throw you in jail if you don't tell them where the dead child you killed is buried. Or you're a slave. Or you stand in a field with a mushroom cloud and think "prepare to die." Or you grip sheets under your chin so monsters who check your bed think you have no body. Kimberly tells the gray-haired therapist that since college she's jotted her dreams in spiral notebooks she still has. She keeps them in her closet, stuffed in cardboard boxes, and even now, even today, she still jots dreams down. She used to struggle up from dreams (they always felt so real!) then read books that assured her people wake up before they dream-die. But sometimes she did dream-die. That happened when I was weakest. Most of the time her dreams were plain old standards like knives, skeletons, monsters and an occasional vampire though once, in year twenty-three, I showed up as a porcelain doll. I had a crack in my body and I held my palm in the air. I whispered (really spooky) "At five years old I broke." Kimberly told her boyfriend at the time about the dream. They spoke of invisible heart but Kimberly later forgot. After the un-forgetting, she saw that boyfriend again. He reminded her what they spoke of and expressed surprise she forgot it. But that's after the un-forgetting, which hasn't happened yet.

When Kimberly yaks about dreams in this room she doesn't make them a joke. She doesn't laugh or brush them away the way she did with family. Her serious words and squinty face get me tight with questions. What if she wants me to breathe? What if I'm wrong and she wants it? When she came back to our body, back from shooting away, she never asked what happened so I knew to keep it quiet. There was a pulse between us, da-dum, da-dum, do you want to know, da-dum, da-dum, don't tell me, but here with the gray-haired therapist, and Kimberly's squinty face, I wonder what to do. Should I, should I maybe, should I take a breath? She speaks again of year twenty-three. She lay on the floor in her acting school yoga class. The teacher said imagine a fluffy cloud. Relax into your cloud. Lie down on it. Let it float. Let the sky move as you release all tension. Feel the softness of your cloud as you let go and

Kimberly dropped from her cloud. She landed in front of a bathroom door cracked very slightly open. When she peeked through the door she saw me, a tangled up girl, streaked in blood, lying by a toilet. I jumped up loud and fast. "Don't you ever come in here, don't you ever ever!" She whooshed back up to the floor, feeling her body shaking, and told herself, "Don't ever relax, there's something very wrong."

Kimberly looks at the gray-haired therapist.

"How strange is that." (Kimberly.)

The therapist smiles a tiny smile to show she's there. There's a long silence. Inside the silence I

171

wonder what would have happened if I'd acted calm in the bathroom instead of going dumpster dog. I could have said "Hi." I could have said "Hey, come on in." That might have spared Kimberly fourteen more years of know/not know. Or might have made us homeless. Kimberly had no money then, and therapy is expensive. Better to stay a locked-up pearl to gaze at under glass. That was the choice I made. Now I worry and think. Should I keep her safe? Do my job? Or breathe and say "come in?" I look at Kimberly in the chair, Kleenex at her elbow, the gray-haired therapist watching. Kimberly seems confused, her mouth is open in question. No words come out, nothing, and the therapist waits in silence. I start to breathe, just a bit, then clamp my mouth shut tight. No. Oh no no. I get it now. I see it. Therapy is a test. All these months and years have been a Red Girl boot camp. Well I won't fail. Won't give in. Won't be fooled by a cushioned chair and a stupid box of Kleenex. I'll breathe if Kimberly says so. She's my boss, my only boss, my orders come from her. I crush myself in invisible heart full of new resolve.

A week later Kimberly speaks of whiners. Whiners are Party Weak with no get-up-and-go. They're burnt marshmallows. They collapse in their own goo of whining whining whining and who wants to be a whiner. Only whiners go to therapy.

Kimberly's wondering now (no, she's not a whiner) if therapy's a waste of time and frivolous as a mud wrap. When she pays her final therapy bill I stretch and laugh and relax. I uncurl myself in invisible heart. Safe. Loose. Proud. Kimberly loves our family. She doesn't need a dead sock. I've done the right thing, I'm sure.

A+ on my test.

Chapter 20
Family Love

Year thirty-two. New York.

I'm still loose and proud. I stay inside the invisible heart, hiding out, doing my job, while Kimberly lives her real real life. She's now on a long dirt road, rural New York, nearing the house, wheelbarrow in the barn. Her legs are moving fast. Her thoughts are whizzing flies. Married in two weeks! It's August. Leaves are green. She yells yahoo while sprinting.

Her soon-to-be-husband is in the yard.

"You got a call." (Soon-to-be-husband.)

"What is it?"

"Your dad's alive."

"But?"

"A heart attack."

"Shit. What do we do?"

"We can postpone if we have to."

Kimberly drives to Delaware. In the kitchen of the new condo she watches our mother shuffle. There's pain in her legs, pain in her back, no it's not getting better. The doctors don't know why. They find nothing, nothing, but what do doctors know. They tell her she's fine when she's not fine, look at her wobbling legs. Kimberly nods her head, forehead scrunched with worry. I've watched this scene before (Kimberly showing worry) but I think, though I can't be sure, that our mother is faking it big time. Not on purpose, no, she believes she's frozen, but she's frozen as a protest, a punch against her life, a punch at me, at Kimberly, a punch at our thoughtless father. This is my theory at least. I don't know what Kimberly thinks. In front of the gray-haired therapist Kimberly spoke of fog. "My mother is a fog. When I think of her I can't see." The gray-haired therapist nodded her head, agreeing that Kimberly's mother, our mother who's now in the kitchen, remains a mystery person. Even to her. Even her. Four long years of listening, hearing Kimberly yak, had not once lifted the fog.

Kimberly helps our mother reach a box of tea. I hear the pulse between them (da-dum, da-dum, I'm sorry, da-dum, da-dum, you should be) as they drink their tea at the table. Our mother has not gone back to the hospital. It's a drive. She doesn't feel safe driving. What she likes is using the phone. Last time was, oh, yesterday? Maybe the day before. But she and our father have talked on the phone. Everything's fine. Everything's fine. Though she's very glad (little tears) that Kimberly's here, that Kimberly can, that Kimberly now will do.

Kimberly calls our father. "Well, it's proven fact. You'll do anything for attention." I hear our father laugh. The heart attack is a joke now. Kimberly knows her job. I clench myself in invisible heart, no longer used to our family, to Kimberly laughing light, la-di-da, la-di-da, and when she offers to drive, to help our mother stand, I start to hold my breath.

When Kimberly lived in Delaware she often said "big duh." Now while driving the car she hears "big duh" in her head. It's a big duh our mother sees the heart attack as something that happened to her. It's a big duh our mother's stiff in the car. It's a big duh Kimberly offers comfort. It's a big duh our mother starts crying and asks Kimberly if she'd ever help her if she had a heart attack. It's a big duh Kimberly grips the steering wheel and says yes.

At the hospital our father is hooked up to tubes. His skin, gray and folded, looks wrong in a pale blue gown. When Kimberly sits by the bed (our mother out getting coffee) she watches the faint, it's very faint, rise and fall of his chest. The hospital lights are bright. His face, a handsome face, looks exposed, naked. Bones shine through his skin, or maybe that's illusion, a trick of the hospital light, but as Kimberly watches him rest, his eyes blue-lidded, fluttering, she can't help but think that our deaths are a breath away. He opens his eyes. Sits up. Accepts a cup of water. Then the story starts. He was downstairs.

Watching TV. His heart jammed up like a fist. It was a crushing pain, you can't believe how crushing. He couldn't move, couldn't stand, he called out for our mother. She was upstairs. Bedroom. She ignored him and wouldn't come down. He hates to say this (he doesn't, I think) but our mother wants him dead.

Would he tell Colin this? Eliza? Jim? Our mother? Kimberly wonders now, silently, to herself, while taking his empty cup. Is she the only one, the confidante, the oldest, the one who understands, the one who hears the mixture, the terrible swirling mixture, of confession, accusation, and finally deep appeal? Save me, save me, she hears from him, she's heard it all her life, underneath the words, underneath the professor, the Party Strong, the daddy, the Captain Grammar who once again, always once again, has landed with the bombardier and joked about cheating death.

"Does Mom really want you dead? Depends if you deserve it." (Kimberly going light.)

Our father laughs, hollow. Then he grips his chest.

"Do you think we should get a divorce?" (Our father gripping his chest.)

Family love is an outline. The body is gone from the scene, no longer there, taken away, but its edges are circled in chalk. The outline lies on a sidewalk, arms out, legs sprawled, exactly as it fell. Detectives stand with pads, taking notes, nothing's clear, but we'll get to the bottom of this. I don't think they will, detectives with their pads, so now, for Kimberly's sake, I step inside the outline. I lie in the borders of chalk. A perfect perfect fit. Dutiful daughter. Dutiful girl. Saving her helpless father. Kimberly feels me there, lying in the outline, lying in family love, so she fits herself beside me. I'm unknown to her, still hidden away and proud, but she knows the lines of chalk.

"If that's what you want, yes." (Kimberly from the outline.)

She offers our father a studio apartment in her soon-to-be-husband's brownstone. She lives in the building, it's theirs, it's where they'll have the wedding, so she'll clean the apartment, furnish the place, do whatever he needs. He can recuperate there, stay as long as he wants, and if it's divorce he chooses, though of course he should see how he feels, he can make the decision from there. He nods his head. Yes.

Back at the condo, sipping tea, our mother speaks of divorce. Should she get a divorce? Should she? What does Kimberly think? Kimberly stirs her tea. In year fourteen through sixteen our mother asked these questions. She'd perch on the edge of Kimberly's bed and Kimberly, half asleep, would answer yes, please do. Now, still in the outline, she offers our mother money. As a child in Nebraska our mother saw hobos on freight trains. They came to the kitchen door and her mother gave them food. Our mother was glad she did, but she's always been, always, afraid of becoming homeless. Divorce might be expensive. Divorce might be too hard. Kimberly offers again. Our mother stares in silence. (Da-dum, da-dum, da-dum.)

Eliza, a CPA, goes to the hospital after work. Jim, recently married, goes to visit as well. Colin calls on the phone, crying youthful tears. Kimberly has siblings. Kimberly could lean. Still, because of the outline, she knows that she and only she can be the special saviour. She stays at the condo for days. She rearranges the cupboards. She tosses old food from the fridge. In the small guest bedroom she cries. She wants our father alive. She wants him at her wedding. She'll be cold in the beaded dress, bought for an August date, but our father can join in October, October's okay, it's all okay (not that anyone asks.) She cries about death and life. She cries about the outline. She cries about speaking of hard divorce instead of her own close wedding. The words of our mother echo. "You don't have to postpone. He doesn't have to be there." After that a silence. (Da-dum, da-dum, da-dum.)

Kimberly, in the casita, drinks a gin and tonic. She puts the glass on a page and it leaves a circle of wet. She wipes the circle with her hand.

"Family love is an outline?" (Kimberly wiping the page.)

"You feel it. I know you do."

"Not so much anymore. They all seem far away."

She stirs the lime with her finger and watches it float like a leaf. Then she downs the drink.

"It's funny though, don't you think? That now you're divorced and they're not." (Me.)

She dumps her ice in the sink. It clatters loud and hard. I see her eyes go blank as she runs her hand through her hair. She lied about the outline. She feels it now. I'm sure. When I write in the casita our life flames up. Close to her skin.

That's the point of un-fearing.

Chapter 21
The Un-forgetting

"Our life flames up. Close to her skin. That's the point of un-fearing."

I wrote these words myself, but they've taken me by surprise. Kimberly's in the kitchen eating beans from a can. Her face looks driven and kind of intense and she hasn't washed her hair. I'm worried she's off her grid. I'm worried I am too. The walls of our casita slant and lean in the night. They seem to be closing in, pressing the words I'm writing, pressing our life with the words, and I wonder if I should stop. Kimberly clatters her can. Her voice calls out from the kitchen but I can't hear what she's saying. I hear the pop of the ice tray. A drink being poured. A curse.

The un-forgetting is next. The un-forgetting was crazy time, my words might flame the crazy. I close my eyes for help. Tikko appears. The bear. They hold a bowl of porridge and drink a sea of gold. "The truth does not use words, it flings them off like acorns flying from a tree." But words are all I have. The bear lifts up his paw. He opens his mouth. I smell his breath. He puts his paw on my shoulder. Keep going, don't stop, keep going.

Year thirty-two. Birth of a son.

Kimberly's very happy, but as a new mother herself, she thinks about our own. Our mother once told her, in year eight, that she won beauty queen contests up through county then state. She quit before trying for state. When Kimberly asked her why, our mother smiled a far away smile. "I wanted to be your mother more than a Miss Nebraska." Kimberly didn't believe this. Our mother, in quiet ways, often gave off the impression, at least in Kimberly's view, that she could have had a fantastic life if Kimberly hadn't been born. Kimberly makes a promise to never give off this impression. She looks at her son, six-weeks old, and tells him she'll keep living. She won't drop dreams then blame him. Not if she can help it. Though she knows she probably can't. Guilt has a trail of its own. It might be part of the outline.

She enrolls in a degree program in playwriting. At the end of three years she's pregnant again and has to write a thesis. The baby swims and kicks inside as she sits in front of her laptop. The thesis is a play, a still unwritten play, so she wracks her brain for a starting idea until I whisper softly. She doesn't know it's me, and I don't know why I whisper, but soon I've become a severed arm found on a beach by a mother. The mother, a panicky type, doesn't know what to do with the arm so she throws it into the ocean. The arm washes back ashore. It becomes a kind of symbol, which Kimberly knows while writing, of why it's stupid to throw a thing into the waves of an ocean. Tides will bring it back. The thing will never leave. After the arm returns the mother goes all mean. She doesn't mean to be mean. It's more like she doesn't know. I try to make her funny, and Kimberly laughs while she types, but the whole time I write this play (help her in secret I mean) she has a nagging sense that she's writing of something forgotten, something she can't name, and it scares her and leaves her tired.

She has the baby, another son. She's happy. Incredibly happy. Until, in year-thirty seven, she sends the play to an agent. The agent sends a response. The agent doesn't "see the humanity" in the mother who tosses the arm, so all good luck but no. Kimberly sinks on her bed, flattened like a bug. I'm sorry for her. Then mad. I think the mother's human. I think she's plenty human. Why does Kimberly believe a stupid agent instead of me? She's on the bed like Party Weak. I'm going to have to push her. Get back up, run run run, come on, get up, get up. She doesn't move. She lies there. I hear her whisper softly. I lean in to listen. I hear her whisper again. "I can't do this anymore." Can't do what, I wonder. She can't hear me wonder, she doesn't know I'm there, but something's opened up. I see her sudden wish (once and for all, she whispers) to find this thing, this shadow, this grip that never leaves, never ever ever, no matter how much she thinks, no matter how fast she runs, no matter how hard she smokes, drinks, dances, smiles or pretends.

She gets up from the bed. She walks upstairs to her office. I watch her open the closet door then pull out the cardboard boxes. They're not marked "Someday" yet. I don't know what she's thinking. I don't know what will happen. She lifts out spiral notebooks. The pages are covered with handwriting that shows time passing. There's a period of circles over i's, a period of slant, a period of straight up and down, a period influenced by the phonetic alphabet she learned in acting school, a period of barely legible. She reads patiently. She sits on the floor letting the words touch her without rushing. In the back of her mind is a swaying ?. I turn the ? upside down and swing on it. I hear the pulse between us, da-dum, da-dum, do you want to know, da-dum, da-dum, don't tell me, and I feel myself swing high, higher higher higher, my ? upside down, the world of me upside down, till I'm sick from swinging, sick, the sickness is fear but I don't stop, sweat flies out of my hair, heart pounding, leaping, should I should I should I, what does she want, what does she want, tell me tell me tell me

Kimberly turns a page. She reads a dream. She turns a page. She reads a dream. She turns a page and reads a dream about a college friend. The college friend says her house was destroyed by rain. All the bed sheets are wet and she can't get them dry. The dream shifts to our mother. Our mother hands Kimberly hot dry bed sheets. In the dream Kimberly can feel the hot sheets in her hands and see our mother's eyes. "These are clean so make your bed." In her real real life, on the floor, Kimberly feels the sheets. She sits on the floor, feeling. She sees our mother's accusing eyes and I make a decision. I jump. I hit the ground. I roll. The invisible heart explodes. Kimberly gets sucked into a vortex that strips the skin off her bones. She sees herself from the outside and inside at the same time as walls of mirage fall like clouds and a slam of instant knowledge hits her in the chest. "My father _____ and my mother knew." She pushes to make it stop, tries to shove it away, but clouds drip loose from her fingers and there's nothing I can do. She crawls on all fours to the toilet. She throws up. She throws up again. She feels naked in snow. She throws up again. She sits on the tile and stares. She stands and brushes her teeth. She sits on the tile again. She begs to please fly backward, back to before, back to before, as I try to say I'm sorry, I'm sorry sorry sorry, but I don't have a voice yet,

Kimberly can't hear. I'm sorry sorry sorry and I kick myself for jumping, I kick myself for the ?. I want to believe I made a choice but I don't know what happened. Kimberly climbs down the stairs. She stares at herself in the living room mirror and knows that she looks crazy. She's jumping around. Shaking. Her whole body is shaking. She's not crazy (I tell her so) but she trembles and shakes and flutters like a leaf inside a tornado. I've caused a swirling storm that twists all sight to string. Funhouse mirror. Step on through. Kimberly steps through the mirror and dangles in the air. The wind of invisible heart throws her to the floor. She clings to her skin, to her hair, she doesn't want to die. Her son and her baby need her. She presses herself against the wind, pressing pressing pressing, until she makes a shape. A hard shape, brittle, but it can hold her for now.

She stands up inside her shape to look at the brand new world. It's laughing and pointing and calling her names. Silly girl! Stupid fool! What took you so long? What took you?

Kimberly's on the casita bed, body under a blanket. She hasn't told me to stop but I'm worried for her so I do. I shove my pages under, and after several minutes hear her muffled voice.

"I'm glad you wrote 'sorry sorry.'" (Kimberly under the blanket.)

"I do feel sorry."

"Yeah?"

She pushes the blanket aside then sits up looking wild.

"How sorry? How much? How big?"

"As sorry as I can be and

"Not enough

"What do you want

"I want to never see you! Ever ever again!"

"Wow, okay, wow. Way to be our mother."

She suddenly pulls me close. She's all contrite and regretful, which I don't trust at all. Then she grips the pages. Her hands run over them lightly, smoothly, softly, slowly, and when she gives them back her eyes look soft and full.

"I may seem off my grid, but I promise I want your words."

"Are you sure?"

She nods her head, hair unwashed and flat. I sit back down at the wooden desk, tired, wanting a rest, then hear her voice from the kitchen.

"We're in this together, Red Girl. The bear is right. Keep going."

Chapter 22
Voice

Year thirty-seven. Brand new world.

Laughing pointing fingers (Silly girl! Stupid fool!) wake us in the morning. Ghoulish echoing wind drags us into sleep. After I jumped from the ? Kimberly feels the hit in her chest but still can't see my face. I don't want her to see me. I don't want her to hear. I zip my mouth, keep it closed, I've ruined enough already. Every day she stares in a mirror, trying to send herself back. Back to the time of outline, belief in the world she knew, or at least the world she thought she knew which has crumpled now like a dream. She stares in the mirror, begging, but there's a hole in invisible heart, all my fault, my fault, I can't be stuffed back in. She holds her brittle shape, fragile, thin, porous, and pulls herself through days. Kimberly can walk, feed her kids, see her friends, hold her mind together if I use the tricks I know. I float from real/not real to give her moments of rest, moments of re-forgetting, where everything fades and all is fine but in the mornings, when she wakes, the hit returns like a fist. Truth. Truth. Truth. I press my hands against it, pushing

pushing pushing, as if it's still a swing, back and forth, know/not know, help me/no help needed, but Kimberly is exhausted.

Her son is four years old now, and she, along with her husband, apply for his spot in school. She sits in chairs, smiling, answering many questions, while ignoring, or trying to ignore, the thought bubbles over her head that are asking (always asking) "Why did I un-forget? Was it sparked by my son turning four? Having a second baby? The thesis play? Nothing?" I keep her thoughts in bubbles, I help her hold her shape, until I'm as tired as she is and make the Laughing Corpse.

I wander the paths of dungeon mind stringing his bones together. Poof, magic, he's here to help. He gives me strength, which I give her, though Kimberly doesn't know. Everything is strange, everything is fear, but the Laughing Corpse can swing me high and toss it all away. At least for a minute or two. A minute is all you need, I learn, to take a step, move, get to another hour. I hum with the Laughing Corpse, sending Kimberly strength, which I could have done for years and years if she hadn't wanted more. Kimberly and her wanting. She couldn't keep me vague, a simple _____ of truth. She had to see the details, had to dig in deep, so she sits on her bed, ankles crossed, and breathes and breathes and breathes till she floats on top of a cloud.

She drops from the cloud, relaxed, then looks at the bathroom door. It's the door she saw in year twenty-three on the floor of the yoga class. Gently now, with a whisper, she asks to see inside. I huddle behind the door, still a dumpster dog. She reminds me that she knows. Reminds me that I jumped. What she wants, all she wants, is a tiny bit of seeing, a teeny tiny glimpse. Could I open the door? Would I? She tells me she won't get mad. She tells me she can stand it. She asks and asks and asks until I crack it open. She peeks inside the bathroom. Sees herself on his lap. It's a slice of silent movie, a quick cut then a blank, but it's enough to send a shock that shudders up her spine. She opens her eyes, gets off the bed, then (I'm sorry) throws up.

This doesn't make her quit. Every day she sits on the bed, forcing herself to relax. I try to resist, try to protect, but I can't keep control. Un-forgettings fly from me and hit her fast and daily. Swings, oceans, headboards. Dirt, bedrooms, lakes. Clothes, closets, bathrooms. Wisp's forgotten room. They spew from invisible heart and they're not dreamy visions. They're a solid punch. Kimberly, when she acted, had used her imagination to inhabit and enter a scene. That's not un-forgetting. Un-forgetting enters you. It wraps itself inside your cells and lives its story hard. Kimberly gets sick. Aching, tired, can't-move sick. Her head's a throbbing melon. Her arms can't hold her hands. She no longer sits on the bed, ankles crossed, breathing. Un-forgettings hit no matter what I try. Kimberly eats a sandwich. Blam. An un-forgetting. Kimberly walks on the sidewalk. Blam. An un-forgetting. I do my best to rein them in but I'm a useless thing. I bury myself in the dungeon mind and cling to the Laughing Corpse. His bones are a vision of light, a vision that I'm loved, so I hold the love for Kimberly and pray she feels it too.

She calls the gray-haired therapist. It's been five years since they talked, but yes, come in tomorrow. Kimberly sits on the cushioned chair, Kleenex in the box, trying to tell our story.

"My father   my father   my

"Take your time."

" _____   _____   _____ "

The gray-haired therapist looks concerned. I don't trust her face. It looks put on, fake, a sugary blob of fluff. I know I'm repulsive. Sick. A thing that stinks a room. She can't fool me, no. She's being polite, taking her pay, holding her nose behind that face, that sugary fluffy face. Kimberly doesn't notice. She pours out her heart to this faker. I try to make her stop but on she goes, yakety-yak, though she speaks in a kind of stammer. Her voice has gone all soft, it's barely more than a whisper, and for weeks and weeks she talks likes this, as if she thinks, really thinks, the gray-haired therapist cares. She doesn't care. No one cares. Kids are little toys that grownups like to break. They don't do it on purpose, grownups aren't that smart, but everything they touch crushes up in pieces. And why can't Kimberly talk right? I'm sick of how she sputters. If she wants to sit in this room, and I don't know why she does, the least she could do is sit up tall and roar like a wild lion. I want her strong. Party Strong. Not all weak and baby, holding that shredded Kleenex, dropping her head in shame. What's she so ashamed of? She doesn't need this room, this gray-haired faker face who says it's not Kimberly's fault. Oh boo-hoo, it's not your fault, well no of course it's not. It's my fault. It's all mine. I'm the one who jumped from ? and ripped the invisible heart. I'm the one who screwed us up and got us stuck in this room. I want to get out. I need to leave. I can't listen to all this talk, this stupid fluffy talk. Kimberly sputters and whispers as if she's some kind of special thing, some person who deserves. She deserves a childhood? She deserves good parents? Oh come on you faker (me to the gray-haired therapist) you can do better than that. We get born. That's it. Everything else is candy. The gray-haired faker knows this. Any moron would. And she knows her words don't help. It's obvious, isn't it? Isn't it? After weeks and weeks of talk

Kimberly's curled in the chair, head down, hanging, fingers limp and weak. The gray-haired therapist leans. She puts on that fluffy sugar voice, trying so hard to fake, and speaks to Kimberly's hanging head.

"Why won't you let me help you?" (Gray-haired therapist faking.)

Kimberly lifts her head. Her face looks haggard and done. Her mouth opens up as if to speak but the words get caught and clogged. She feels me rumble inside her, a huge impatient rage. She opens her mouth again and my voice roars out of her throat.

"I'm dead trash! Already dead! Nothing helps if you're dead!" (Me.)

I'm stunned by the words. Stunned by my voice. I don't sound like a friendly kid, I sound like a low dark scream. A strangled motor. A crazy howl. Kimberly jumps from the cushioned chair, Kleenex still in her hand, and the sound of my voice pours out of her mouth, roawwwww roawwwww roawwwww, tomcat in the dark, coyote on a kill, dead trash rising wild, swirly, spooking me out, spooking all of us out.

Kimberly falls to the floor, bent and under attack. She punches her fists and kicks her feet to fight what's happening now, what happened to me in the past, and she screams and rolls and skitters the floor, begging for _____ to stop. I shoot up to the ceiling and watch her scream and skitter. I want to be shocked and horrified but all I feel is cold. Mean. Harsh. Sadistic. I'm the empty monster. I'm happy with Kimberly's pain. Now she knows. Now she knows. That's the way it was, that's the way it felt, and now I get to shoot away, now I get to watch. I'm calling it love, calling it love, while Kimberly sprawls on the floor, strange, lost, embarrassed. She sits up finally, still on the floor, and looks at the gray-haired therapist.

"Wow. What the hell. My body is taking over." (Kimberly.)

She grabs a Kleenex from the box after crawling herself to her chair. She's in a kind of stupor. Exhausted by my voice, exhausted by her body. The gray-haired therapist looks concerned (this time I believe it) and tells her next time, when she comes, to plan for a double session.

We start daily sessions. A double when it's needed. For weeks my strangled motor voice roars from Kimberly's mouth. The gray-haired therapist sits, eyes clear, watching, as Kimberly flails and roawwwwws. When she stops her wild flailing Kimberly tries to go calm. She presses her feet on the floor. Ground yourself. Press your feet. Find the present moment.

Once, during a session, she wonders aloud, jokey voice, if there's a place to go for a peaceful dreamy cure. She'd like to sit in a big white chair that rests on a lush green lawn. The lawn will slope from the beautiful doors of a calm and elegant castle. Nurses will carry trays. The trays will be silver and drinks will be brought, along with a draping blanket, to the white and numerous chairs. Voices will murmur if wanted. Silence will reign if preferred. Kimberly will sip, cool, delicious, fresh, and feel the cacophony lift, the craziness drain away, the many un-forgettings flow through the tended plants.

"Hardly a psych ward description." (Gray-haired therapist smiling.)

"Yeah, I know, I know." Kimberly laughs a tinny laugh. "I'm in wishful thinking."

While she laughs her tinny laugh I jump to the dungeon mind.

"You're not a sadist." (Laughing Corpse.) "Don't even bother to ask."

"But I'm on the ceiling watching. All I feel is cold. Mean. Harsh. Hateful. I don't want to be like him."

"Like who."

"The empty monster. Make me a better person. Save me, please. Fix it."

The Laughing Corpse looks unsure. Then his eye sockets sparkle.

"Tap my bones. Use them."

I play a tune on his ribs, plinging them with my thumb.

"Play it louder Red Girl."

I pling as loud as I can. He tells me, while I'm plinging, to use his bones to hear myself. I'm sturdy love, a spirit thing, a strength that I can hold. When trouble comes my way, which trouble often does, use the plinging tune.

"It's always with you, Red Girl. You can trust it always.'

"And Kimberly?"

"She can too."

I pling more bones to thank him. Then I leave the dungeon mind full of wild hope. Kimberly sits on the cushioned chair, still in wishful thinking. The gray-haired therapist talks. Kimberly's doing okay. She's hanging in, the path is rough, but a hospital setting? No. Kimberly's got a spirit. Kimberly's got a phone. Call whenever, anytime. Take some baths. Get some rest. And call, yes, whenever. Kimberly thanks her and leaves. She stands on the sidewalk still as glass while Broadway traffic weaves. Then she hears a tune. She hums along, wondering how, but glad for the pulling sound, the tune I plinged on ribs. At home she runs a bath. She fills the bath with bubbles then drops her body in. The sound of my roawwwwwing whispers up, ringing through her ears. She knows I'm her, but how. How can a hidden howl, a shard of know/not know, float inside a self like an embryo wrapped in cloth. She hears her background murmurs. "Help me help me," is there, a child's voice, trapped in a well, calling out from her mind, and "You'll die if you don't shut up." She turns their volume up, lowers it, turns it up. The sounds are echoes of past, etched in the grooves of brain. She imagines her mind as an ant farm. Jim had one on a shelf, in Delaware, on a shelf, where once (she closes her eyes) she watched the ants move grains of white, watched the ants go crawling, watched and watched and watched before she shot away, before she had to, no. She slides down into the tub, holding her head underwater. She'd like to open her brain, let the bathwater flow, slosh the ant farm, wash it away, a do-over mind, a whole new thing, wouldn't that be a beauty. She blows from underwater and listens to her bubbles. Where does memory go? Who or what can see it? Maybe we sit as a dust mote, a speck of irritation, on the eye of another world. Maybe we're metaphor only. Maybe we're thought. Pieces of time. Maybe we're plinging tunes. She rises out of the water. Bubbles hang from her body, foam of an ocean wave. She brushes her skin with a towel. She sees the translucent nature, the melding into air, of the edge of her arm, her leg, her skin as her baby whoops downstairs. His stroller has come through the door, his brother walking near, and the sight of home, the hallway, has burst him into glee. Kimberly dries her hair, smooths her face in the mirror. The running of feet (her four-year old son) and the sound of her baby whooping pull her into life, out of ocean, out of foam, into the smile of effort, into the carrying on, we carry on, we carry, we carry our love, we carry.

Kimberly paces near the desk, creaking the boards of casita floor while looking at the words. Her eyes scan back and forth and she's still pretty intense. I ask if she wants to swim. Hike. Ride the bike. She snaps at me (still intense) then tells me not to stop. Our time in Taos is halfway up so go, come on, let's go, un-fear the invisible heart.

"I'm writing as fast as I can." (Me speaking the truth.)

"Well there's no time for hiking."

She heads off toward the bathroom where I hope she'll wash her hair.

"Yes, I'll wash my hair. I'm not that gone, I'm really not, I just

She stops for a moment.

"I like the plinging tune. Thanks for giving me that." (Kimberly.)

"It was the Laughing Corpse."

Kim Merrill

Kimberly steps into the shower. I hear running water and the sound of her terrible singing. I try to block the sound as I start up writing again.

Chapter 23
Lola and Wisp and Little One

Year thirty-seven. Where I left off.

Kimberly goes to sessions, takes her baths, holds her shape, till one night she can't sleep. She hasn't been sleeping much, not since the un-forgetting, but tonight her mind starts pounding. Her husband's in London (meetings) and her sons are asleep upstairs. She leaves the bedroom, sleepless, and her body, that brittle shape, seems about to slither.

The living room shines with brightness. She knows she's tired, slithering, strange, so she tries to ground herself. Find the moment. Find it. Find the present moment. She wanders the living room now, touching the sofa, chairs, mirror, bookshelves on the wall. She says out loud what they are. "Sofa. Chairs. Mirror. Bookshelves on the wall." Except that's not what she says. She hears a voice that's not her own bubbling out of her mouth. "Divan. Chaises. Miroir. Les livres pour ouvrir." Why is she speaking French? She doesn't remember French. Not the way she's speaking now, in a child's voice, high and light, lilting, confident, oui, tres bien, un bon accent, mais quoi? Kimberly touches her lips. "Pain chocolate, gribouille, je veus je veus je veus." I clutch the shreds of invisible heart, now in a rising panic. I whisper in Kimberly's ear, trying to stop the terror. "We're in your living room, Kimberly" (me whispering in her ear) "a brownstone, Upper West Side, New York City, United States, earth, galaxy, universe, I'm here, you're here, we're here." Except what comes from my mouth are high pitched nursery rhymes. "One-two, buckle my shoe, three-four, shut the door, four-five, who's alive." Kimberly skips like a three-year-old then drops herself on the sofa.

She opens a book of photographs. The book is large, an art book, and Kimberly enters a page. She wanders through the hills, walks inside the print. She knows she's me (I tell her so) and she can feel it herself. She's reading as a child, words stretched out and real. I watch her close her eyes, desperate to leave the book. Try to sleep, try to sleep, try to go to sleep. In a brief and twilight sleep we hear our mother's voice. "We can play some Candyland." Kimberly and I (feeling ourselves as one) move pieces on a game board, Candyland with our mother, till Kimberly's eyes jerk open. Her heart pounds with a fear. Has she ever hurt her sons? Her brain goes into swirl, racing now with questions. If she forgot her life, her childhood, our _____, could she forget her sons? Could she have hurt them? Should she check? She rises from the sofa, ready to run upstairs. Then she sits back down. She's too unsteady, too unreal, too terrified of herself. She doesn't think she's hurt them, she sees herself as soft, but tonight, this night, this slithering night, she can't trust her mind.

Kimberly clings to the sofa. Hold on, hold on, hold on, strength, focus, courage. She stares again at the book. We enter a page and climb a tree. We hide behind the leaves. We peek from the tree then see ourselves. Kimberly and memory sitting on the sofa. Yes, we're cracking up. Something's breaking, something's here, I can't make it stop. I stay on the sofa with Kimberly while both of us stare at the book. Morning will come. Morning will come. Morning will

Then a ripping. Little One, Lola, Wisp and myself burst from invisible heart. I can't describe this, don't know how, but we charge out into the room like Pueblo chaos clowns. Except our skin's not painted. We have no skin at all. We're holograms. Spirits. Shards of identity. Shards of time. Our voices call and speak. We're born of invisible heart, born of the shooting away, which Kimberly knows, I know it too, but still we shake in shock.

"Who are you?" (Me to them.)

"Je suis petite, I read in a tree, give me a puff of that."

I look at the swirling shards and Kimberly's face wide open. I need to grab her mind before it's gone for good. "Kimberly!" (me shouting.) I shake her body steady and tell her I have a plan. I have no plan, I'm lying, but Kimberly wants to believe. The swirling shards of herself laugh and swish and point. They fly up high on the bookcase, throw themselves at the mirror, dangle from the lights. How can shards of self fly around a room? Kimberly looks a wreck. She's lost her shape, lost herself, but then, and this is a punch, we recognize the voices. French, Hoosier, wiseass. High pitched, flat, laughing. They sound distinct and different, not like me or her, but we've heard them before, somewhere, murmurs in the brain.

Kimberly's eyes start begging, begging me for help, so I zoom through my nonexistent plans and remember the Laughing Corpse. "If trouble comes" (this is trouble) "use the plinging tune." I jump to the dungeon mind and break off one of his ribs. In the living room I pling and pling while Kimberly touches the sofa, touches the chairs, touches the mirror, touches the wooden bookshelves. Hours (or maybe minutes) pass in a kind of trance. Then, and who knows why, the shards drop down from the ceiling and rest on the living room floor. I look at the three of them sitting. Kimberly looks at them too.

Their faces are hers and mine. They're us in a kind of mirror.

"What do you want?" (Kimberly.)

"We want you to know our names."

"Tell me." (Kimberly brave.)

"Je m'appelle Une Fille Petite. In English call me Little One."

"My name is Wisp."

"I'm Lola."

"And me, my name is Red Girl."

Kimberly presses her hands on the floor to keep herself from shaking. The five of us speak together, taking turns, telling. Little One, Wisp and Lola each hold spans of time. They gave me what they forgot and I kept it all on my ledge. They're happy to meet me now. Happy to meet each other. Happy to be together after so many years in invisible heart, crouching, deep, secret, and now, finally, here. Knowing this is scary. Knowing this is real.

"You need to fall asleep." (Lola to Kimberly kindly.)

"Can you help me?" (Kimberly.)

"You'll sleep if you introduce us." (Little One.)

"Tell that gray-haired therapist who are are." (Wisp.)

"Tell her what happened tonight." (Lola.)

Kimberly nods her head. Anything, she'll do anything. She calls a friend (she knows it's late) could the friend come over? Would she? The friend arrives at midnight. She tells Kimberly's sleepy sons (they wake on her arrival) that everything's fine, everything's fine, but she's going to spend the night, their mommy needs some help. The friend crawls into Kimberly's bed and Kimberly curls in a ball. I don't remember any of this, the friend tells Kimberly later, but I do remember what comes before. Little One, Lola, Wisp and I tell Kimberly her name.

"Clueless. That's what we called you. You were always Clueless."

Chapter 24
Bones of Family

Year thirty-seven. Same night.

When Kimberly falls asleep, Little One, Lola, Wisp and I jump to the dungeon mind.

"Look what burst from invisible heart." (Me to the Laughing Corpse.)

The Laughing Corpse looks surprised.

"Do I have to love them no matter what?" (Laughing Corpse.)

Lola peals a laugh.

"I got no need for a bag of bones. Though you do look kinda familiar." (Lola.)

She sways her hips as she walks, then strikes a match on his cheek. He takes her hand, swings her, they dance while she puffs and laughs.

"God it's great to be free!" (Lola really happy.)

She kicks off her shoes to celebrate then races across the stones. Little One climbs on the Laughing Corpse to jump from the top of his head. Wisp plays the ukulele, tapping her foot near a tree, then all of us spin in a circle while the Laughing Corpse cackles in song.

"What took you so long to get here?" (Laughing Corpse.)

"We had to knock through Clueless." (Wisp.)

"She means Kimberly." (Me.)

"Kimberly's clueless in every way. No idea, all these years, that we've been running her life." (Lola.)

"Clueless dummy!" (Little One.)

The Laughing Corpse looks confused.

"It's called dissociation. A big ass word for fear." (Lola.)

"More than fear." (Me.)

"Don't get parsey, Red Girl. We're secrets behind a wall and the wall is made of fear. If Kimberly hadn't been Clueless, we could have been here all along and

"I'm the one in charge. She's Clueless because of me." (Me.)

"Well la-di-da to special you." (Lola.)

"I'm not special. I'm a jerk. I didn't do my job. Kimberly feels a horrible pain that's all my fault, all my fault

"Red Girl, no. It's not your fault." (Laughing Corpse.)

"And I wasn't trying to blame you." (Lola.)

I can barely hear their words as I choke in stupid hiccoughs. I don't know what's wrong with me. Maybe the night before, maybe the stress, maybe fatigue, maybe the wave of change, maybe the

"Can you hear me?" (Laughing Corpse.)

I wiggle my hand as yes.

"Give me invisible heart. It's too heavy and hard to hold

"It's mine, I have to

"No. Everything's not your fault and everything's not your job." (Laughing Corpse.)

I can't believe his kindness. I give him the formless invisible heart and he spins it on his finger.

"What kind of hat do you want?" (Laughing Corpse to Little One.)

"Peut-etre un beret." (Little One.)

He flips the beret on his head. "Handsome, don't you think?" He turns his skull from side to side as I feel myself go light. I hadn't known how heavy, how pressing, how exhausting. I raise my arms in the air and jump up like a rocket.

"Promise you'll always keep it." (Me.) "I don't want it back."

The Laughing Corpse nods his head then strums his ukulele. "Nobody likes me, everybody hates me, guess I'll go eat worms." All of us sing along (except for Lola smoking) and after the song is finished he breaks off all his fingers. He gives a pinky to Little One, tosses a thumb to Wisp, Lola grabs an index.

"These are bones of family. Red Girl needs a family." (Laughing Corpse.)

We pling a chorus on his ribs and I'm the happiest ever.

Kim Merrill

Kimberly hears us in her sleep (I make sure she hears) and in the morning, when she wakes, she thanks her friend. Hugs her sons. Feels their warm close skin.

Chapter 25
What to Believe

Year thirty-seven. Next morning.

Kimberly walks up Broadway. She sits in the cushioned chair, Kleenex in the box, and coughs up little whispers.

"There's something I need to tell you." (Kimberly.)

The gray-haired therapist nods. Kimberly tries again.

"I don't want to sound crazy, but, um, yeah. Last night I went into this bizarre, yeah, I'll call it bizarre, cracked up kind of state where I had to promise something that sounds…..well, crazy."

I remind her (now in silence) that the invisible heart is real. As real as the cushioned chair. As real as the box of Kleenex. She speaks again more clearly.

"I was in the living room. I opened my mouth and rhymes came out. One, two, buckle my shoe. The pitch of my voice was high and I started dancing around speaking French. I don't remember French. I was saying things I no longer know and I felt like I was breaking. I tried to make it stop by looking at a book. I entered the pages. Kind of. I mean that's how it felt."

Kimberly pauses. I nudge her to say what she came to say.

"I couldn't stop all the French and nursery rhymes that came out of my mouth. Then, and I'm not sure how, four pieces of me appeared. They made me promise to tell you."

The gray-haired therapist leans forward in her chair. Kimberly exhales.

"There's Little One. She's around four or five and has a really high soft voice. When I'm with her I feel terrified."

Kimberly's voice is high and soft and terrified. Her voice changes.

"There's Wisp. She's in fourth and fifth grade in Indiana." Her voice changes again. "There's Lola. She's a sass bomb who makes me laugh. She doesn't give a shit what anyone thinks. She's pretty angry though." Her voice changes again. "There's Red Girl. She's the one with that low dark sound we've been hearing in sessions."

Kimberly looks at the gray-haired therapist.

"Do you hear my voice changing?" (Kimberly.)

"Yes."

"I'm not trying to do that."

They sit in a stillness.

"I'm really scared." (Kimberly.)

The gray-haired therapist leans back in her chair. She puts her hands together and holds them to her lips. Then she puts them down.

"I need to say something too." (Gray-haired therapist.) "I've never seen this before. But I consult with a mentor and describe our sessions to colleagues. What I hear from them is yes, your experience sounds like authentic dissociative memory."

The gray-haired therapist pauses. Then she leans forward.

"I can't tell you what's real or not. What I can tell you is that I've never, and I say this after checking with my colleagues and myself, suggested anything or put ideas in your head."

Of course she didn't. I'm not stupid. I made sure to jump only when Kimberly said so. I pulsed the pulse between us, da-dum, da-dum, do you want to know, da-dum, da-dum, don't tell me, and the truth is mine and mine alone. I start to get mad in the room, thinking of all I've done. The dreams, the clues, the notebooks, the holding of breath in invisible heart. I'm about to start a rooawwwww until I hear Kimberly speak.

"Thank you for telling me that." (Kimberly to the gray-haired therapist.)

They spend the next month dissecting me. Can I be trusted? Believed? What am I? The gray-haired therapist listens as Kimberly talks of reasons, reasons to trust and believe. Last week she saw an old boyfriend who was visiting New York. When she told him she un-forgot he reminded her of the dream she had, back in year twenty-three, where I showed up as a porcelain doll and whispered really spooky. She had, according to him, "talked about it" way back then when they were still together. Seeing him again has stirred up the real/not real. The real/not real she carries around. That she's getting really sick of.

She adds to her list of reasons the notebooks she wrote in for years. A notebook from year thirty-one spells it out on the page. How did her mind forget? How does a mind erase? Or not erase, it didn't erase, it placed behind a curtain, a curtain made of gauze, a billowy curtain of real/not real, now you see it, now you don't, now you're a crazy liar. Kimberly wonders why she's not sicker. Shouldn't she be a drug addict? Homeless? A self-cutter? Her life seems uneventful, placid, boring, plain. How can she believe the shrieks of invisible heart? And yet they keep arriving. Louder and louder and more and more and what about Wisp? The forgotten room?

The gray-haired therapist speaks of Wisp. Wisp's un-forgetting was vivid, re-lived and seen in this room. Watching Kimberly then-as-Wisp gave the impression, in her view, of something that could have happened. Maybe not every detail, there's no perfect recall, but, again her impression, quite difficult to dismiss. Kimberly always remembered "Your mother almost died and you lie there reading a book." She always remembered "What do you want me to do?" What she forgot-then-un-forgot was being lifted. Taken. Into a room. A forgotten room. A room where she typed I hate hate hate and thought, while un-forgetting, and said, while un-forgetting, "I want to kill my father. I want to write him dead."

Kimberly puts her head in her hands. When she lifts her head she speaks.

"I'll go to Indiana. I'll look for the house. Look for the room. Look at the whole damn town."

The gray-haired therapist opens her mouth and I jump to the dungeon mind.

"Wisp!" (Me screaming in dungeon mind.)

All of them race to help me. They pound on my back and lift my arms until I blurt out words.

"She's going to Indiana. She wants to test me, test me, I can't have her test me."

"Calm down." (Wisp.)

"Can you guarantee the room?" (Me.)

"No, of course I can't

"Then what then what then what

"Pull yourself together!"

Wisp jerks away and climbs a tree. She sits on a branch, watching, while Lola pours me a drink.

"Try this." (Lola.)

I down the gin and tonic and feel myself get tipsy.

"Give me invincible heart." (Me slurring to Laughing Corpse.)

"I can't, you made me promise

"I need to pull out facts! There's gotta be something in there, something left inside. Proof, a magic wand, a piece of miracle, piece of pie

"You're not making sense." (Little One.)

"There's no proof in invisible heart. It's hard, but that's how it is." (Wisp.)

"I want her to believe me! I have to prove it, have to prove, have to make her believe!"

My tipsy pathetic voice leaves me in a puddle. The Laughing Corpse pulls me up and sits me on a stone.

"Does it really matter?" (Laughing Corpse.) "You already know your truth and no one else will care. They'll always call you crazy, so why waste time with invisible heart? Why not re-forget?"

"Re-forget?"

"Sorry."

The Laughing Corpse backs away from the rising rage in my face.

"I can't re-forget. Even if I could, why would I ever want to?"

He swoops me up on his shoulders and sits me there unsteady.

"Take the invisible heart. It's yours, of course, so take it." (Laughing Corpse.)

I feel the cord between us (love, trust, bond) that pulls me toward his kindness. There's no proof in invisible heart. Wisp is right, I know she's right, as much as I wish she wasn't. I lift my hands from the flat beret and slide myself from his shoulders.

"Can we forget I did this?" (Me really embarrassed.)

"What happens here will stay here." (Lola winking a wink.)

I slide myself back to the therapy room (still a little tipsy) and listen to Kimberly's words. She's animated, listing, adding to the reasons. Once, in Central Park, sitting under a tree, our father snapped at her three-year old son. "If you don't stop that whining we're leaving you here alone." And once, in the upstate house. "If you don't stop your talking I'm throwing you over that beam." When her three-year old son started crying, Kimberly patted his head. "Oh, that's grandpa joking." Now, on the cushioned chair, Kimberly speaks of her own year three and jokes that were never funny. Why did she let him scare her son? Why did she not speak up?

The gauze of real/not real kept her then from seeing, kept her then from knowing, that our father could be an asswipe. And she saw it with her eyes. As an adult. Just last year. So maybe the un-forgettings, the horrible un-forgettings, could be true, true at core, who knows, who knows, who knows, but the months of crazy shrieking, the appearance of me, Lola, Little One, Wisp, seem to her now (don't they to you?) a kind of fact, a kind of thing, with no other explanation.

Except the truth. Being true. Or an alien invasion. Or a snatching of her body. Or past lives, that could be it. Maybe the un-forgettings belong to a medieval princess. Or a Chinese girl with bound up feet. Or maybe

"Our time is up." (Gray-haired therapist leaning.)

"To be continued." (Kimberly laughs.) "After I come back."

Chapter 26
The Letter

Year thirty-seven. Manhattan.

Before the Indiana trip Kimberly writes to our parents. She doesn't want to sound angry. Or hysterical. Or delusional. She sits at her desk and types (deletes and types again) for three long difficult days. She describes the facts. Describes the past six months. She asks if they would answer a few questions. She asks if they would go with her to family therapy. She asks they not tell Eliza or Jim or Colin about the un-forgettings until she's told them herself. She makes a copy of the letter. She puts it in the cardboard box. She proofreads the original seventeen times. She proofreads her signature. She folds the letter and puts it in a stamped envelope. The letter is three pages of single-spaced typing. It's stapled and signed with blood. That's a lie. It's ballpoint pen. The heartbreak feels like blood.

Kimberly seals the envelope. Then she decides, heart pounding, to write some words on the seal. "This letter contains upsetting information. Please don't read it alone." Kimberly doesn't want our father to have another heart attack. Or our mother to faint. Or a floor to open up. Or a world to explode and go shooting into another orbit.

She holds the envelope. She walks to the intersection of West 78th Street and Amsterdam Avenue. She turns north on Amsterdam. She opens the blue mailbox at West 79th Street. Prayers she doesn't believe in fly from her cold chapped lips. She stands in the space of do and don't. Do it. Don't. Do it. Don't. Do it. No don't do it. She slides the envelope into the blue mailbox. Her eyes fill with hot dryness as she shuts the metal door. She looks north, south, east, west. She's done a thing she can't undo and her pale and bloodless body needs a place to rest. She wanders around the streets. She stops at the door of a church. She opens the door. She enters. She smiles at a man who approaches her to ask if she needs help. She does. She would like to sit in silence, alone, here, now. He nods and leaves her alone.

Her knees lean on a pew bar. Her palms fold. Her brain splits. Two translucent hands reach for her from the sky. They pick her up. They lift her. She feels the lift and sees herself, rising up in the hands, hands of god, of heaven (oh, if she could believe) and knows she's watching a death. A death of who she was before she sent the letter. A death of who she'll be after the letter is read. She's dry-eyed. A surprise. She expected tears, not this terror nothing. She sees herself in the hands, lowering now, lowering. She steps from the hands. Grateful. She has her limbs. Her blood. Her vision of being lifted.

She thanks the man in his church. She opens the heavy door and walks out on the sidewalk. She goes home. She makes dinner. She sits with her two sons. She memorizes their faces. She packs a suitcase. She falls asleep with her husband. She dreams (she may have dreamed) of the trip to Indiana. Fly in a plane tomorrow. Find the forgotten room. Find what's real/not real. Find whatever she can.

Chapter 27
Indiana

Year thirty-seven. Indiana.

The sun shines pink as Kimberly drives. The highway is flat. The fields are flat. Wisp is with us now. She flutters invisible in the car (here/not here, heard/not heard) as Kimberly watches the road. Wisp and I look at drifts of snow roped in furrows of dirt. We're waiting for the mountain and castle frothed in moss. We remember that hope from years ago as we worry about the letter.

The letter is in a balloon (we decide to imagine) riding a steady breeze to Sanibel Island, Florida. That's where our parents are. Retired. Trying it out. Jim and Maria (Jim's wife) live in Florida too. The family seems far away (Delaware for Colin, Eliza in Pennsylvania) and also close, so close, as if they're in the car. Wisp and I worry together about the un-forgettings. The facts. The forgotten room. The terrible test of me. Then we shake our heads. Kimberly has to drive. Pay attention. Stay alert. We can't distract her now.

She checks into the campus hotel. It's close to empty. Winter break. The sky in the window is gray. She puts her suitcase on the bed. She drops her head to her knees. Wisp and I wait nearby. In spite of our presence (she feels us there) she thinks of Manitoba province in Canada. The bullentin board in the classroom said Manitoba was one person every ten miles. For a moment she's one person every ten miles hitting the head of a dead snowman. She watches it twist, around and around, the wooden tetherball pole. Then, on the hotel bed, she thinks of being alone. She couldn't be here with someone else. Her mind couldn't roam the years (only two years, remember) of living in this town. Where's the playground? The school? The U-shop? Stadium? Woods? She has no iPhone now (they're not invented yet) so she has to rely on me. She thinks of how I am. I loop and whirl and scatter myself like snow on a faraway hill. I show a snapshot picture, a swath of color, a smell of soap, I rarely connect a dot. I'm bad with time (What year? What day?) and tend to wander paths that may or may not end. Everyone's memory does that. That's a lie. We're all unique. Kimberly has a friend who can't forget a single thing he's ever read or eaten. People's brains compute. Create. Confer. Confirm. Why is she stuck with me? A drifty dreaming type, a girl with her head in the clouds?

Snow is falling down. Kimberly goes to the hotel desk and borrows a black umbrella. She slogs to the campus library (it's not far at all) and browses through archival microfilm, news clips, old directories. She sees the name of a man who visited us in France. Here's another name. (Who's this?) Here's another place. (What's that?) Here's a blurb about the church. I kick my shoes against the pews (Eliza, little sister, Eliza, little sister) while Kimberly reads and understands that the church belongs to the college, a place of worship and place of work, way back then, maybe now, oh and what does it matter. Kimberly rubs her eyes. She's straining (she's been here for hours) to glean some understanding. Of what. Really of what. Our father? Our family? Our life? She should sleep, get some sleep. Tomorrow the snow will stop (if the weather report is true) and we'll walk the town in sunshine. We'll find the playground. School. U-shop. Stadium. Woods. We'll find the house on Hanna Street. We'll see (or not) the forgotten room. She opens the black umbrella (now having stepped outside) and watches her boots in slush.

Wisp and I race through Kimberly's brain. We wade through folds of memory squealing oh look, look there. When Kimberly falls asleep we dream a wonderful dream. We stand at the door of the Hanna Street house. A beautiful woman appears. She smiles and says come in. We follow her trailing gown up the stairs, wooden stairs, until we reach our bedroom. Eliza's bed is unmade. Mine (Wisp's) is perfect. Comanche stands on the floor with Barbie in his saddle. Rocks with veins of gold lie inside a shoebox. Wisp and I toss a rock down the stairs. It bounces on each step. The beautiful woman follows the rock. She picks it up, holds it, then lays it on a table. The table is in the forgotten room. On it are papers and look, oh look. A typewriter. Yes. Electric. A typewriter. Yes. Let's write him. We kill our father slowly (banging on each key) until he's words (no skin, no blood) and the beautiful woman laughs. We're brilliant children, she says. We should get perfect grades.

When Kimberly lifts her head (the clock alarm is buzzing) we race away and hide. We stay in the folds of brain, more confident now, more certain, as Kimberly stumbles for coffee. There's a pot in the room for brewing. She inserts a plastic tray then sips from a paper cup. She showers. Dresses. Puts on her shoes. Now we're in the sun.

We take her to Martha's house. Is that it? We're not sure. Could be. Could be not. The day will be like this (could be/could be not) but we feel at home on the streets, the broken jagged sidewalks, the trees with winter branches. We walk to the public library. Wisp often read her books, open in her hands, while trying to stay on the sidewalk. Now we walk with eyes held up, looking at signs, buildings, the stretched out lack of height. We forgot how flat it was, trees instead of city, and we enjoy the sky. It lightens Kimberly, lifts her up, Wisp and I can see that. We try to leave her alone, let her look for herself, but the folds of memory spill us. We walk across the campus. We see the diagonal paths and remember ourselves with sticks, holding them tight, racing, twirling them like batons. We dragged them behind us, tossed them, played as if on a playground which is where we're heading now. If we can find it. Yes, we can. There's the school. There. Hershel Shelton's mouth crunches a grasshopper leg. Martha pricks our fingers, we're blood sisters now, sisters, and yet, looking today, it's empty swings and flatness. That seesaw, was it there? Or is it new, what's new? We walk on the roots of a tree. We balance lightly, jump a bit, wave our arms like birds. We step on the dirt (it's frozen) and walk back through the campus.

We pass the U-shop (empty of ducks) as Kimberly tries to remember. What was she years ago? Skinny legs. Homemade clothes. A dress of green. A ribbon. Our mother sewed our dresses. She remembers her Barbie, the homemade checkered coat. She remembers pigs, the smell of them in trucks. We find the college stadium, the walls we jumped and walked. They're narrow now, so narrow. In front of the woods we used to roam is an exercise path with stations. Pull up bars, ramps, a stretch of painted tires. There's outlines of faceless people (handless and footless also) who show you what to do. Follow the arrows, chin the bars, hop inside the tires. We crash behind the asphalt path through trees and branches and brush.

Kimberly sits on a mossy rock. She pretends she's skinny. Braided hair. Homemade dress. She remembers the time she noticed. Sitting still, on a rock, she noticed she was alone and then decided not to. Kimberly wants to notice now. Wisp and I agree. We sit on the rock. We touch the moss. We let our minds cascade.

We notice a fear inside us. It flattens the air. Pulls us away. Pins us under glass. We hear the sound of typing keys, our father working at home, clattering clatter clatter. A guilt swims in our body (oh so very familiar) as we worry about our father. Working hard, typing, lost in restless thought.

We hear a laptop typing. Kimberly's letter now. Was it correct to send? We fear we'll hurt our father. Hurt ourselves. Hurt the world. We're not that big, we know this, but sitting here on the rock, touching the moss, smelling the dirt, we still feel afraid. Why are words important? Why does a tongue insist? Kimberly typed three pages, single-spaced, careful words, "Please don't read it alone." And for what? For what? To explain herself? Insist herself? Why can't she stay quiet? Kimberly grips the moss, hands suddenly tight. Who cares what family thinks. She doesn't need a family. She doesn't have a family. She has a family outline (mother, father, siblings) that wraps her in lines of chalk.

On the rock, cascading, a surge of anger flickers. Wisp and I wonder what to do. Notice her anger? Not?

"I vote notice." (Wisp.)

We jump ourselves to dungeon mind and pick through anger stones. We lift a pearl, big as our palm, and toss it back and forth. Then we drop it down. We want to find the perfect size, the perfect one to give her. We find a dark green pearl no bigger than a pebble. We carry it from the dungeon mind and place it at Kimberly's feet. She picks it up to look at then feels a heat rise up. Her heart begins to bang. Her skin begins to pop. We watch her eyes go flashy. Sparks of light and fire shoot inside her pupils. She bites her lip. There's blood. She clenches her hand in a fist and pounds it against her leg. Then she throws the pebble. She doesn't want to feel it. She swallows her anger down (she's an expert at this) and bites her cheeks, holds her breath, until her heat goes cold. She shivers inside her coat.

The gray-haired therapist told her (has told her many times) that she hasn't touched her anger. She's able to cry, roawwwww with sound, but anger doesn't come. The word empowered is used.

Kimberly hates the word. Her anger never ever (ever ever ever) delivered a touch of power. It was laughed at. Walked from. Spit on. Called a joke. It ended in helpless sobbing. Begging. Pleading. Silence.

"That's okay." (Kimberly.) "It's all okay for now."

She stands up from the rock, wipes a scrape of moss. She walks to the exercise path. She climbs a ramp. Steps on a tire. Hangs from a chin up bar. Then she sits on a bench. Her mind (with the help of that pearl) wanders into revenge. She's never been one for that. This morning, at the hotel, she picked up a local paper. In a nearby county, not in this town, a woman lifted a shovel to smash her mean old uncle. She's in custody. He's half dead. Both are from a family where no, they never guessed it, none of the neighbors saw. That's anger. That's revenge.

Kimberly can't see the point. Or maybe she's kidding herself. Maybe a shovel would do it. But what does she really want? Not blood, not guts, not shovels. She typed a letter, single-spaced, to extend a hand, express a wish, for love, counseling, hope. Yes, pathetic. Saccharine. Good girl outline, good good girl, but what is she really after? I lie back down in the outline (visiting for a moment) and hear a tiny wish. She wants to hear "I'm sorry." She wants a family who says it. I look at Wisp, she nods her head. She wants "I'm sorry" too. We know it doesn't come. But a girl can dream (Kimberly laughs) and want a magical thing.

She walks to the only restaurant. She orders a burger and cheese-fries. While she waits she reads the ads on her grayish paper placemat. She could buy a tractor. She could get a haircut. When the burger comes (here you go hon) she sees a couple enter. They sit in the booth one over. It could be/could be not the Cavenish parents from next door. They're wrinkled now, hair is white, but the shape of them both (a wish in her mind?) is the Cavenish mother and father. Kimberly feels a sudden urge. She wants to lean toward the mother, smile and ask politely "Did you really call me stuck up?" Of course she doesn't do this. She sits in a strange amazement, a glow of warmth and shock, that a possibility sits, close, one booth over, for her to mention the shed. The Orphan game, cleaning the shed. Did they ever see, did they ever (if they're willing, now, to answer) a reason to wield a shovel? From their window? Porch? Did they ever hear Kimberly, as a kid, express a quiet dread?

They order macaroni and a heap of beef stew special. Kimberly wipes her mouth, needing several napkins. She can't do it. She can't ask. She can't slide from her booth, stop for a moment at theirs, and ask, politely of course, if their last name might be

Cavenish. She feels unmoored enough. Flattened. Pulled. Fearful. She should pay her bill.

Outside, queasy and warm, Kimberly walks to Hanna Street. She postponed looking this morning. Now, late afternoon, the sun will set in no time. Better find it. Hurry. She swings her arms at her sides and strides with urgent purpose. She'll find the house. Poke in the yard. If someone's home she'll knock. Her heart starts beating hard. Her fingers twitch in her pockets. She's now that little kid, a little bare legged Wisp, scurrying home from school. She's thinking of Girl Scout badges. She's talking to Abraham Lincoln. She's skipping and running then quieting down. No more football in the yard. No more running hard. Our mother has pulled her aside. "You can't be playing with boys." She misses throwing the football, as badly as she threw, and she misses chasing Jim. Touch, not tackle (well, tackle sometimes) and sliding through the grass. The grapevine in their way. Make it a goalpost. No! We want the grapes alive!

She stands in front of the yard now. She knows the yard. The football game. There's the scraggly grapevine. There's the slab of concrete. The slab where the play, her first, was staged in a single day. Except the house is gone. There's no house. Nothing. She takes a breath. Dies inside. Just a little death, she'll be fine, she'll be fine, but now, in the empty field, tromping the empty field, she walks an outline of the house, crushing it with her shoes.

She's making the outline up. There's no way to know. The house was demolished, burned, hit by lightning, moved on a truck, pulled up by a tornado, years ago, years ago, why oh why and she cries a bit, a tiny little hiccough, a strangled cry of shit, goddamn, this is crappy luck. The other houses are here. There's the Cavenish shed. Should she knock on their door? No. They're still eating (if that was them) and even if they aren't, she's in no shape to speak. It'd be stupid to try. It'd be stupid to stand here. It'd be stupid to type, single-spaced then send, a letter to our parents. Asking for it, asking. She's a stupid waste. She's a moron walking.

"No you're not." (Wisp.)

Wisp holds out her hand. Kimberly stares at the dirt. I look at the two of them in the field and wish I could fix it all.

Chapter 28
You Must Be Crazy

Year thirty-seven. Manhattan.

Kimberly's in the hallway, back from Indiana. The hallway's crowded with toys, a stroller, her coat, her shoulder bag, her pale and ashen face looking from the mirror. She holds Eliza's letter. The writing swims like eels. "You're sick, disgusting, get some help." She stuffs the letter in her bag and feels her stomach punched. Our father sent Eliza, Jim and Colin too, copies of her single-spaced signed with blood three pages. She had hoped he would do as she asked, let her tell them first, let her tell them herself, but why would she hope, why would she hope. She knew when she stood at the mailbox (Do it. Don't. Do it. Don't) that she was a surefire goner.

Our father's letter is typed. Single-spaced, same as hers. It details the desperate state of Kimberly's fragile brain. A brain that's under attack. That's been touched by some kind of fabulist. An egotistical therapist or blossoming mental disorder, we can't know for sure, but the family hopes, truly prays, that Kimberly gets it fixed. He's attached, for her perusal, studies on suggestion. Perhaps she read a book that ruffled her sense of self. Or got herself hypnotized.

Or simply needs attention. There are people in need of attention who grab at victimhood. There's comfort in the victim game, if the victim has been unhappy. Frustrated, maybe. Despondent. In search of something to blame. Has Kimberly been unhappy? Frustrated, maybe? Despondent? If this is the case, she's forgiven. We all fall prey to suggestion. We all make errors of judgment.

More and more letters come. Many with studies attached, research about the brain. It's an epidemic. There's a florid growth of delusion born and nurtured and tended in the heat of imagination. Therapists need the money. Victims need the love. Accusations hurt. Accusations shatter. So many innocent parents, so many broken lives. Look around, you'll see it. People make shit up. People do whatever. There's no justice, none at all. Thoughtful people see this and Kimberly's always been thoughtful. Such a bright girl she was. Always asking questions. Always a healthy skeptic. Use your head. Think. Come to your goddamn senses.

Kimberly writes replies. She defends me (not enough) with articles of her own. She explains that her un-forgettings come from her, just from her, her very own life and mind. They aren't hazy, dreamy, they slam her into the floor. Each re-living a terror. Each new time a scream. Can he understand? Can he? She doesn't want disruption, she doesn't want an exile, but she can't, she simply can't, call herself crazy, call herself nuts, call herself deluded. She loves the family, please know that, please know she's in pain, but she won't ever, ever, pretend and lie again.

I shake my head in disgust. These letters back and forth, copied, studied, analyzed, tossed in the cardboard box. Where's her pride? Where's her rage? I'd be a flaming dervish, a spitting mouth of war. I'd kick and swirl and kill him if only she'd let me type. But of course she won't, she never does, she keeps me in control. Her control, hers, and I never get to attack, rip up his words, shred them, call him a twisted liar. I'm the one who's truth. I'm the one in danger. Kimberly should fight. Type her fingers bloody. Or not even type at all. Throw him in the trash. Make him feel like me. Dead. Gone. Ripped. She plunks her head on her desk. Her shoulders shake and tremble. When she raises her head there's streaks of tears drying around her mouth.

"It's possible, you know, to miss a person who scares you." (Kimberly to me.)

I jump myself to dungeon mind.

"Lola! Little One! Wisp!" (Me.)

They race to my side, ready.

"Can you miss a person who scares you?" (Me.)

"Do you mean Daddy?" (Little One.) "I miss Daddy."

"I do too." (Wisp.)

"Yeah, I guess I do." (Lola.)

"Why? What do you miss?' (Me.)

Their eyes cloud up with thinking.

"I miss the daddy who laughed. The one who taught me to read." (Little One.)

"The daddy who hiked and sang." (Wisp.)

"The man who said I was bright. Who said I should never give up. Who said I should follow my dreams." (Lola.)

"Who carried me on his shoulders and never let me fall." (Me shocked to hear myself.)

They look at me and nod. A daddy can hurt and sing. A daddy can hurt and love.

I miss him badly now and see, I suddenly see, that I held a tiny belief he wouldn't lie. Wouldn't dismiss. Wouldn't smack me down. Mental disorder. Victim. Seeker-of-attention. I thought he loved me (how could I think?) and I thought I had a chance. Stupid stupid girl, stupid moron walking.

"No you're not." (Wisp.)

"He likes control, who doesn't." (Lola.) "All you can do is run. Or suck it up if you have to."

Lola lights a cigarette. She smokes it halfway down then stubs it out on the Laughing Corpse who's snoring like a geezer.

"Wake up guy." (Lola.)

He lifts himself to sitting and wobbles his heavy head.

"It's this hat, this invisible heart. It wears me down, puts me to sleep, but have no fear, I'm here." (Laughing Corpse doing his best.) "What happened? You all look awful."

"We miss Daddy." (Little One.)

"He's calling us sick." (Wisp.) "So is the rest of the family."

"Big duh and no surprise." (Lola.)

The Laughing Corpse touches his jaw, looking really thoughtful.

"Maybe he doesn't remember. Maybe he really can't." (Laughing Corpse.)

"Come on, what a crock." (Lola.)

"Dissociation, sweetheart. Bad ass word for fear. Didn't you say so yourself?" (Laughing Corpse.)

"Yeah, but

Lola stops. She swoops up Little One onto her hip and takes Wisp by the hand. They wander away, leaving me there, alone with the Laughing Corpse.

"I want my truth to be heard but not at the price of family." (Me to Laughing Corpse.)

"That's an impossible wish."

"But if he can't remember, doesn't know what he did, what does that do to me? I can't get angry or punish if he really doesn't know. But I don't want to be crazy girl, dreamer, little liar. I won't do that, I won't, so how do I

"Red Girl, stop. It's only the human brain. Which has its problems, don't you think? At least in your situation."

I stand for a moment, speechless. I trust the Laughing Corpse but his words are pretty cold.

"That's all you have to say?" (Me.)

"That's all that can be said."

"Then go back to sleep." (Lola returned.) "Go back the hell to sleep."

I don't stay for the rest of this, as I now hear Kimberly's laptop. She's typing more letters, I'm sure, so I jump away from the dungeon mind, thoughtful and contrite. I understand her now. She's in a war of reality and wants to win with words. She thinks if she can find one, the perfect perfect word, our father will surrender, will magically pop and change. This doesn't happen, of course. The Laughing Corpse is right. The human brain has problems. That's all that can be said.

Chapter 29
Our Mother

Year thirty-seven. Manhattan.

Another letter comes. Careful rounded cursive. Unbelievable words. Our mother (!) will help us. She'll answer written questions about the un-forgettings. Don't though, tell our father. She doesn't want him to know.

I grab a piece of paper. I throw it on Kimberly's desk. Together we draw pictures. Pictures of clothes we un-forgot. Clothes that showed our ages. Clothes that showed location. Clothes we saw in flashbacks but don't know if we owned. Dresses, ruffled shirts, a furry dog applique. Daisy pants, ladybug socks, a corduroy jumper, a coat. Next to each picture we draw a ____. A fill-in-the-blank. "Yes" or "No." "Yes" for yes if we owned it. "No" for no if we didn't. We make up some clothes we never saw. In instructions we type for our mother (yes, we're that controlling) we explain that "Yes" or "No" will not mean she's confirming. There's made-up clothes in the list. A safeguard. Way to assess. So answer as best you can (Yes/No, Yes/No) and we'll be (now we're crying) very very grateful.

We stop and think. We wonder. Do we ask about the van, horseback riding, arms cut off, the strange and scary and please-not-real Los Angeles un-forgettings? Kimberly doesn't want to. Our mother is skittish. Fawn like. If we push too hard, ask too much, she could dart away. We decide to ask one question. About the living room. Beverly Hills. Where friends of our father gathered (maybe, maybe they did?) while Eliza lay in a hospital bed trapped in walls of white. A man we un-forgot brought a bucket of chicken. We rained the crumbs on our tongue. We danced and twirled and all the rest but we keep this out of the letter. We ask our mother simply (as if there were such a thing) to tell us, if she knows, of men in the living room. Beverly Hills. Anything she can tell us, anything at all, will (and we cry again) be very very helpful.

Now the Hanna Street house. Would she draw, would she mind, a simple sketch of the floor plan? Label the different rooms? We don't mention the reason. We don't mention tromping the field, crushing it with our shoes. We mention our wish, our hope, and again, we're very grateful.

Kimberly signs the letter. Copies it. Goes to the closet. She opens the cardboard box (still not marked with "Someday") and drops the copy in. She walks to the intersection of West 78th Street and Amsterdam. She turns north on Amsterdam. She opens the blue mailbox at West 79th Street. She stands in the space of do and don't. She slides the envelope in. At home we wait. Try to forget. Put it out of our mind.

I'm nervous (so is she) and startled to see (I didn't know) that I don't want to be real. I don't want to be true. I want to go back to Daddy. Mommy. Daddy. Mommy. I want to be a liar. Dreamer. Crazy kid.

We wait and wait and wait. We wait for several weeks. We stand in the crowded hallway (shoes, toys, stroller, her ashen face in the mirror) and sift through piles of mail. We sift and sift and sift. If email was common (it isn't yet) we wouldn't have to sift. We wouldn't wait and wonder and oh. Oh no no. Here it is. Oh no. Our mother's rounded cursive stares at us from the center, right smack there in the center, of a recycled paper envelope, stamped with a little tree, a holiday stamp from Christmas, the Christmas Kimberly missed this year, the year of un-forgetting.

She puts the envelope down. Picks it up. Puts it down. Picks it up and holds it. She goes upstairs to her desk. We look at the envelope, now on the desk, and it seems to glow and stretch. It covers the desk, covers the walls, covers the earth for a moment. It's not that big, we know this, but the envelope, not yet opened, holds for us both (yes, both) a quivering jumble of fear, a world in an open hand, a life on the edge of real/not real that we don't want to topple. Kimberly uses her teeth to tear the envelope corner. She slides her finger hard across the envelope's length. She takes out our mother's letter. Opens it. Lays it out. She runs her hands on the creases to flatten it on the desk. She stares at it unseeing. It takes some time (for both of us) to watch the writing smooth itself, quiet its wiggling wave.

Kimberly's eyes are dry and bright. She points to the fill-in-the-blanks. The clothes un-forgotten marked "Yes." The clothes made-up marked "No." Men in the living room once. Our mother came home from the hospital (once, only once) to a group that had been drinking. One of them yes, that's right, was the friend who brought over chicken. She asked the guests to leave. It was getting late. Hope the sketch is okay. Hope you can read her writing. Kimberly looks at the sketch. The floor plan shows, in ballpoint pen, the rooms of the Hanna Street house. "Dining room." "Kitchen." "Bathroom." Next to "Living Room," there it is, Wisp's forgotten room. "Office then Colin's Bedroom." Kimberly covers the page, hand shaking and hot. I lift her hand, wanting to see, needing to see again. We stare at the page together. "Office then Colin's Bedroom." Typewriter. Crib. Oh no. Oh no no no no. I'm real. I'm here. I'm true. I'm Little One. Wisp. Lola. I'm

Kimberly shot from her body. I'm the stink of dead sock and trash in a can and I don't want this, no no no

Kimberly folds the letter. She sits for a very long time. She picks up the phone. Puts it down. We can't call our mother. Last time she hung up. And the time before. And the time before. But I know our mother answered once, cried, hung up, cried, hung up, and once, then once again, stayed on the phone and talked. The calls all blend together and words bob up in bubbles. Bubbles of thought, bubbles of words, da-dum, da-dum, I'm sorry, da-dum, da-dum, you should be, da-dum, da-dum, da-dum, da-dum

"Mommy, please, Mommy." (Kimberly trying not to cry.) "Help me help me help me

"Stop it now. Stop." (Kimberly in the casita.)

Kimberly's at the wooden desk. She's wearing a dirty bathrobe and her face is all puffed up.

"I can't stand what she said." (Kimberly looking upset.)

"But we have to un-fear it

"Do we?

"That's what you've been saying

"Then give me the pencil

"Oh

247

"Give me the goddamn pencil before I bust a vein."

Kimberly grabs the pencil and writes with terrible speed.

Title of Book: _Words My Mother Said_

Favorite Part: _None_

Least Favorite Part: _I knew when you were older. I didn't when you were a child. How come you never told me? I waited for you to tell me. I wanted you to say it. But you never said a word. It's too late now. Much too late. I decided long ago I couldn't leave a marriage. Marriage is forever. Marriage is a choice. He told me that you liked it. He told me it was you. And no one believes a wife. No one would believe me. Now it's not my problem. It's all your problem. Always was. Now I'm hanging up._

Draw A Picture From The

Kimberly throws the pencil.

She jumps to the single bed and yells "Oh fuck it fuck!" She hurls a pillow. "Fuck it!" She goes to the bathroom mirror and stares at her streaky face.

"Why can't we be normal?" (Kimberly looking desperate.)

"Um, because no one is?" (Me trying to be helpful.)

Kimberly bursts out laughing. In spite of herself she knows me, and likes to laugh when I'm right. She sits on the bed still laughing then takes a breath and exhales.

"'I knew when you were older?' What kind of batshit is that?" (Kimberly.)

"At least she made me real."

"And I'm glad for the confirmation. I mean as opposed to nothing. But I wish she could have

"Yeah I know."

Kimberly goes to the kitchen and pours a gin and tonic. She sits with it for a while, slowly taking sips.

"I guess it's pretty normal. Denial, I mean." (Kimberly.)

"Yeah, I guess it is."

"And there's nothing we can do."

"Not that I can think of."

Kimberly toasts me with her glass then fills it up again.

"Should I keep going?" (Me.)

"What?"

I wave the pencil. She squints at me with blurry eyes (I think she's getting drunk) then rubs her thumb on her forehead. Her head goes nodding up and down and I take that as a yes.

Chapter 30
Visiting Jim

Year thirty-seven. Still in shock.

After our mother's letter facts may bend and twist, hover inside their ?s, but when they do we hold the words "I knew when you were older."

Kimberly visits Jim. He lives in Florida now, having moved there with Maria. Maria's from Puerto Rico and their house, designed by them, has a swimming pool inside.

"I love the water." (Maria.)

Kimberly stands in the pool. She and Jim are alone. Maria's on an errand and took their young son with her. The water laps and swirls as Jim and Kimberly speak.

"Here's what I remember." (Jim standing in the pool.) "Sounds from your room in Delaware then seeing you in the hallway. You'd sleepwalk up and down, all around the house. Wait, you don't remember?"

Her face must have looked surprised.

"No, I guess I don't." (Kimberly.)

"We'd talk about it at breakfast. We laughed at how you'd sleepwalk, roaming around the house. Then you'd tell your dreams. These really horrible dreams and yeah, I used to worry. You were always tired and you were always laughing. Like nothing was ever wrong, except I knew it was. I swear I thought you were faking. I didn't know you forgot."

Jim goes quiet and swirls his hand. A circle of water ripples. Kimberly looks at his hand and wants her mind to leave. I pull her back in time, back to happier years. The lake in Maine in the rowboat where Jim smacks a fly (we see the welt) and we feel the elusive love. Where we ride a bike, standing, Eliza on the seat. Where we flip ourselves through air. Go to school. Study. Chalk on the board. Chalkboards. The tent in Europe, running fast. Telling our Duckberg stories. Eliza making chocolate cake when Kimberly's sick with mono. She knows we love a chocolate cake so she sits on our bed, knitting, she's been learning to knit, and watches us eat her chocolate cake while we say "Thank you Eliza." The short trapeze outside. Our mother calling us in. Spaghetti for dinner tonight. We sit at the table, six of us there, laughing and laughing and laughing. The dog (his name is Luke) has grabbed a chunk of bread from Colin's feeding hand. Colin has gotten nipped, not hard, a little, enough to swear, enough to fling his napkin. Luke is racing away, Colin running after, all of us laughing and laughing. Our mother does a tap dance on the kitchen linoleum floor. Our father raises a glass, he's so proud of our A's. We hit and miss a tennis ball, over and over and over, with Jim (very good at tennis) patiently saying ok, let's try again, let's try. Now, back in the pool, Kimberly hears his voice.

"Though I don't want you to think that I can really accept this. I knew in a know-but-not-know way and I can't go against dad. I don't know how you can stand it, living without a family."

Kimberly can't really stand it. But she knows the truth of our mother's words. "It's your problem, always was." She looks at Jim. His face is pinched. Kind. Caring. Trapped. She touches his arm in the pool. She'll be okay, her touch says.

"It's not like I like it." (Kimberly.) "But thank you for talking and having me here."

"Maria thought we should. One of her relatives

"Yeah, she said

"Had the same

"I know. It's really not uncommon."

They leave the pool, dry with towels, eat the dinner Maria brings and smile at Kimberly's nephew. He's four years old. Looks like Jim. Tomorrow Kimberly's sons will come. They'll all have a one-day visit, she and her sons and husband. Maria asks her now, eyes full of understanding, what she might like to do.

"Oh I don't know." (Kimberly.) "Maybe a drive to the beach."

Kim Merrill

Their day at the beach is shovels and pails, sandcastles built, drinks in cups, children running from waves. Kimberly watches her family, her sons, her husband, herself. She says goodbye in her mind, quietly, softly, sadly, to her parents. Her nephew. Jim. Maria. Colin. Eliza. She lets them drift away, wordless, gone, drained, water seeping in sand.

Chapter 31
Dog with a Bone

Years that follow. Manahattan.

After the day at the beach, when our family seeped in sand, Kimberly never betrays me. She could have decided to play along, call herself crazy, call me a liar, call me a big mistake. She doesn't. She stays her course. Our father, after some years, finally stops sending letters. Our mother never calls. Neither do Colin or Jim. Eliza, after a decade, breaks her silence and comes to New York to see one of Kimberly's plays. After that they email, once a year, briefly, on each other's birthday.

Kimberly works to heal. That word means I don't know what. How do you know when you're healed? When nightmares stop? Flashbacks fade? You start to know who you are? None of these things ever happen in the first ten years of work. But Kimberly tries, she dogs it out, she's nothing if not relentless. Stubborn. Focused. Get it done. She applies herself to healing as if she's learning a trade. She reads every book, tries every trick, studies the inner workings of her jangled broken self. All for a sense of completion, of reaching a light in a tunnel, which doesn't come and doesn't exist (that's what I try to tell her) but she keeps at it, dog with a bone, chewing with bloody gums.

She takes us to a group the gray-haired therapist finds. The group will last eight weeks. It's free for victims of crime. We realize, when we hear this, that we're a victim of crime. We never called it crime, we called it growing up, but Kimberly likes the word victim. The word survivor doesn't suit, though she understands, of course, the attraction of the word. For her (she says to the group) "survivor" implies a hero, a fighter, an overcomer, but that can become a goal post, a marathon run, a judgment, and where's the shame in victim?

The group is only women, all of them with a _____. Some prefer survivor. Some don't really care. Each is on a path. Each is on a journey. Each is a kind of lonely guest on a casually guided safari. The leader assigns us dates. One date for each of our stories. Hearing everyone's stories will show us we're not alone. There's comfort in knowing you're not alone.

Kimberly doesn't feel comfort in knowing she's not alone. She gets sad for all the kids. All the kids. All through time. It must be human nature, must be the human brain, which has its problems, don't you think, and that's all that can be said.

Still, Kimberly tries. She tells her story to the group. She listens intently to others'. She tries and tries and tries to feel herself healing up, finding that comfort inside a group, finding that thing, that ring of brass, that will prove she's not a victim, oh no no, no victim, she's a warrior woman, she's a winning survivor, you go girl, go go go. Some days it seems silly. The constant work, the lookouts, the crushing waves of flashback. She wants to quit, go to sleep, seep her life in sand. She doesn't. I won't let her. I pling the ribs of the Laughing Corpse to keep her going, keep her alive, keep her wanting more.

"Can justice ever exist?" (Kimberly to the group.)

They've been speaking of jail. Revenge. Hitting with shovels. And do the perps remember. Or do they really not know. None of the women in the group has tried to punish her family. Family can be an outline (Kimberly says this now) that keeps us held, keeps us bound, keeps us wrapped in silence. An aching grab of tribe that shames the one who breaks it.

What Kimberly wants is "yes.' A clear and open and said-aloud expression of crime and regret. A Socratic kind of reckoning, or confession, if you will, where guilt is defined and claimed and lifted from a body. This is an ideal world, of course, but wouldn't it be a lovely thing, a chance for clear renewal, if our _____s could be acknowledged, all the many _____s, and then, oh then, well we all know, all of us sitting here, that there's no reckoning, really, for crimes that are denied.

The group looks out from their chairs. Nodding heads. Clicking tongues. Kimberly knows they understand (all too well, she thinks) her wish for an unheard "yes."

"But we live in the world. The world's unfair." (Someone in the group.)

"See you next week same time." (Group leader.)

Years later, after the group, Kimberly tries something else. She holds two buttons in her palms that vibrate back and forth. Back and forth, back and forth, and this is to push me back and forth, swing me into a part of brain that consolidates and narrates and makes a story of words. This back and forth is called EMDR, and Kimberly does it for months, but all that really happens is deep and frequent headaches. Later, after more years, she tries another technique. She sits with memories (me) and feels them deep in her body. She's very good at this, she knows now how to feel, but I'm supposed to dissipate, shed myself from her nerves, and still I stick around.

I often wonder who she'd be if I could up and leave. Maybe she'd be the same. A plodding dogged type, hoping to feel alive, hoping to wake like a gong. Or maybe she'd be different. Someone who could know herself. Say "that's me, that's not." Hold her head up. Know what she wants. Know how to go and get it.

But she lives with who she is. She helps two sons grow up. She goes to a mountain and learns to ski. She learns to ride a horse. She goes to rehearsal where actors perform and learns to rewrite her plays. She notices pockets of happy. She breathes them in for joy. She's lucky. She's very lucky. Her feet can move. Her body can breathe. Her mind can imagine dreams. She puts her attention on all these things while I set out to stalk her. I shoot flashbacks often, especially during success. It's like I want to sabotage every good thing she does. I hold her under a thumb, crush her dreams, her sense of self, her belief in having choice. I don't know why I do these things but I'm stubborn as a germ. I'm a lot like her.

She doesn't look back (well not that much) at the family who seeped away. She swears she's fine without them except on special occasions. Birthdays. Thanksgiving. Christmas. Mother's Day. Father's Day. Other days. She knows these days are only dates, blanks on a calendar, humanly marked, and time is bigger than that, time doesn't even care, but still she feels a pull toward traditions of being home. Thanksgiving at Eliza's, their house in Pennsylvania, where Kimberly chopped the onions and Eliza whipped potatoes. Christmas trees in

Delaware, everyone reading their poems. Mother's Day calling her mother. Father's Day calling her father. Hearing the voices of childhood, the people who knew her, knew her mistakes, knew her beautiful times. Who knew she had to get stitches after trying to rescue a turtle. Knew the broken rowboat. Knew she held the eel. Knew she hated mustard and loved to eat chocolate cake. Knew marshmallows on a stick, sharing them burnt and hot. She doesn't look back (well not that much) but she carries a quiet wish, an unspoken private wish, that someday, maybe someday, things will change, a call will come, a shift and offer of hope.

"Wait, hang on, wait." (Kimberly in the casita.) "A shift and offer of hope? That's not true. That's not right. You forgot the phone call."

"Phone call?"

"Yeah, the phone call. The one where I stopped hoping and knew it would never change."

"Oh, I remember now!" (Me not sure I do.)

"What's wrong with you? What's going on? How could you forget that?"

"I'm really good at forgetting. It's what I'm trained to do."

"No, it's more than that."

Kimberly's drinking gin. Too much gin. Way too much. I start to ask a question but she leaves the casita. Slams the door. I know she needs to think so I give her plenty of time. She watches the racing dog spray up twigs and leaves. She runs her hands through her hair. She walks outside the casita, thinking, I see her thinking, while her mouth goes open and closed. When she comes back she pours more gin then puts her hand on her hip.

"You're the one holding the hope. You want me holding it too and that's why you forgot." (Kimberly.)

"What are you talking about?"

"You paint with a rosy brush and live in imagination. That's got to stop. Right now."

"What's wrong with wanting hope?"

"Nothing, if it's real. But hope for getting that family back is la-la-la and crazy. I want reality, Red Girl. I want you to write me real."

"What about me?"

"What about?"

"I'm writing invisible heart the way I really lived it. Yes, imagination. Yes, my little head. Don't go all realistic, I'll die of death and boredom."

"What?"

"You know what I mean."

Kimberly puts her hands to her face. I'm sure she's had enough of me, I can tell by her hands. They're twitching and tapping her forehead as if she's about to explode. I sort of enjoy what I've done.

Kimberly gets so dogged, so ploddy and conscientious. She needs me (I now decide) for sparkle and illusion.

"No, I don't want illusion. I want to find out what's wrong with me." (Kimberly.)

"There's nothing wrong."

"Red Girl. I'm in a casita writing with you. I'm drinking too much gin. I could be outside. I could be living a life. Instead I'm obeying a bear. A bear who's not even real."

"We can't know that for sure."

"Would you just

"Yes, I will. I'll un-fear the call."

Chapter 32
The Phone Call

Year of the phone call. Manhattan.

Two planes have rammed Twin Towers. Kimberly doesn't know. She's walking through Central Park with a notebook in her hand. The notebook belongs to her son, he forgot to take it to school, and the air is bright with fall so Kimberly's walking it over.

She stops at the edge of the reservoir, the northern edge of the water, to watch a thread of cloud. It's barely visible, way downtown, and looks like a cut in blue. At school the eyes of the entrance guard are blank when he takes the notebook. There's a lull in the air, something's off, as she walks back home through the park. She sees a woman on a bench staring into space. She hears a man, jogging, scream "Oh my god!" on a path. He stops, breathing hard, headphones still in his ears. When she asks what's wrong he shakes his head, tells her the towers are hit. Nothing known, nothing yet, all he heard is jumping, people jumping out, he's quitting his run, leaving the park, some kind of shit's going down.

Kimberly races home. She turns on the TV. Thread of cloud. There's that thread of cloud. She tries to call her husband (he's upstate this week) but her cellphone doesn't work. No one's cellphone is working. The sidewalks fill with people lining up to give blood, buying water, buying food, pushing strollers, clutching pets, trying their phones again. She heads back through the park to get her kids from school. The school is swarmed with people, some are crying, some are stern, some have slipped inside a glaze that keeps them from collapsing. After several hours she holds the hands of her sons. They talk on the sidewalk outside school then walk through Central Park. The air is completely quiet, except for the buzz of the hanging things, the helicopters, yes, they're hanging above to guard us. From what, oh I don't know, murmuring to her youngest, hand gripped in his clench. I don't know, I don't know, but we're going home together now, we're walking, there's no buses, but when we're home we'll, I don't know, play some games, stay inside, wait for I don't know.

Time blurs and gathers. No cell phones. No way to reach. People on the sidewalk lock their eyes with strangers. They now understand the world. A thing can happen. Anytime.

After several days (or less, I can't be sure) the cell phones return. Service restored. The school her sons attend gets several random bomb threats. When it re-opens (after a week?) Kimberly rides her bike to smoky streets downtown. Orange cones. Barriers. Trays with souvenirs. Little flags, buttons, curling paper maps. A smoke so thick it hurts and yet, we're all assured, safe to breathe, we're safe to breathe, everyone keep breathing. In the news there's lots of stories. People are reaching out, from everywhere, around the world, to reconnect with far flung friends and family in New York. Grudges are getting patched. Misunderstandings forgiven. Swells of love and gratitude and thankful to be alive. This might be exaggeration. The stories might have been few. But they stay in Kimberly's mind as she listens to the message.

Jim is talking with urgency.

"Kimberly, this is Jim. I think this is still your home phone? Please call, please, we've been worried and trying to reach you."

Kimberly looks at the phone. She and Jim haven't spoken (not since the day at the beach) but she wants him to know she's okay. She calls his home in Florida. She hears a woman's voice.

"Jim and Maria's house." (The woman is our mother.)

Kimberly hangs up the phone. She stands above it, dizzy. There's a pounding in her veins. Her skin feels like an oven. She goes to the sink, rinses off, wonders what to do. The voice, she thought, was recorded. But that doesn't make any sense. It was our mother. She answered the phone. She's at Jim and Maria's house. Now what. Now now what. Kimberly shakes a finger (this is inside herself) and gives a good talking to. "Call again. Do it. Do it for Jim and Maria." She holds the phone in her hand. She stares at it for a moment. She presses buttons quickly.

"Jim and Maria's house." (Our mother sounding recorded.)

"Is Jim there?"

"No, he's out. May I tell him who called?"

"Mom. It's me."

I remember silence. Kimberly taking a breath.

"Jim asked to know if I'm okay. So that's why I'm calling."

"Alright. I'll give him the message."

"Okay and

Our mother is gone. Kimberly puts down the phone. She goes to the sink again (the phone is in the kitchen) and hears the voice of Lola. "If she can't care when your city is smoke she's never gonna care." Kimberly washes her hands. She rubs them hard with dish soap and rearranges words. "I'm glad to know you're okay." "I was worried too." "I saw the smoke on TV wow it was quite a scene." Anything but the silence. Click of the phone. Hang up. Kimberly dries her hands then holds a towel to her face. She feels her hope disappear.

She gave our mother gifts. Little childish things. Handkerchiefs she embroidered. Poems she wrote on paper. Every gift she offered was met with strange distraction. She wonders now (towel on her face) if something's wrong with our mother. Not with herself. Our mother. She decides, no she doesn't decide, the choice is made, it happens, that she'll give up forever. No more quiet wishing. No more pointless hope.

"Yeah, that's the phone call." (Kimberly in the casita.) "Thanks for doing it right."

Her face is small at the kitchen sink. She's drying her glass with a paper towel while squeezing her eyes tight shut. She drops herself on the edge of the bed then shoves her feet in her boots.

"Because, and I think it's important, we have to accept what's real." (Kimberly.)

She ties her boots from the edge of the bed while thinking about our parents. Eliza will call or email, Kimberly hopes at least, if our mother or father dies. Not if they die. When they die. They're old, our parents (how old now?) so any day, any year, she might hear. If she hears. If Eliza calls. She wonders what she'll feel. Maybe a surge of relief. Sorrow. Empty space. Maybe nothing at all.

Kimberly stands from the bed. She puts a pencil and paper and a lighter in her backpack. We hike the winding trail and get to the throne at noon. She sits on the throne of jumbled rocks then pulls out the pencil and paper. She gives me a serious look.

"Write our parents' invisible hearts." (Kimberly.)

"What?"

"I'm sure they have them."

"Yeah but I've never seen

"Write what you can imagine."

"But

"Just take a stab."

I spread myself in the dirt. I look at Kimberly waiting and do my very best.

Title of Book: *Inside Our Mother's Invisible Heart*

Author: *The invisible heart*

Red Girl's Stab At Its Words: *I am a wondrous miracle the mind creates for itself. I am the place of no escape where the self explodes and shatters. A mother is a piece. Kimberly's mother split in two with loving and disliking. She loves her daughter sometimes but most of the time dislikes. Her own ma did the same. Scolded with floured hands. "Pa is only jokin'. Don't you mind that man." Kimberly's mother skates alone on a river in Nebraska. Up and down the river loving it when it froze. She gets her picture taken. She could make some money with the beauty that she has. She does the beauty circuit.*

She makes it through to state. She won't try Miss Nebraska. She gets married instead. Her pa delivers mail. Hobos come to the door to get a plate of food. When her pa meets her fiancé he spits into a cup. "So you live in New York City. I hear there's lots of Jews." She marries to get out of town. She has a girl named Kimberly because she wants a family or birth control has failed. Her ma and pa don't visit east but she goes back sometimes. Her small town paper prints her name every time she does. She goes to the funeral of her pa. Doesn't go to her ma's. Her ma lived in a nursing home and when she passed it was just too hard, too much going on, to get out there for what. To say goodbye to a box. No, she wasn't needed. Not sure even wanted. Marriage is a promise. It yokes you to something big. Rules. So many rules. Cook the egg. Serve it. Look the other way. Hold a dream inside or maybe let it go. Be a mother. Be a fawn. Be a stretch of Nebraska plain with blue eyes sharp as fear. No tongue tells a truth. No hand calms a brow. Now she doesn't walk right and doctors don't know why. She's scared of why she freezes. Scared of her oldest daughter. That daughter smokes on the street. Only sluts do that. Maybe she's too hard on her. Maybe too darn soft. It's hard to know with daughters. You're better off with a boy.

I hand the page to Kimberly then push myself to the next.

Title of Book: *Inside Our Father's Invisible Heart*
Author: *The invisible heart*

Kim Merrill

Red Girl's Stab At Its Words: *I am a wondrous miracle the mind creates for itself. I am the place of no escape where the self explodes and shatters. A father is a piece. Kimberly's father split in two with loving and empty monster. Sometimes he loves his daughter but most of the time he's empty. His father dies of a heart attack. He's sent to school that day. Thirteen. Go to school. His Swedish immigrant mother can't raise a boy alone. She's gone Christian Science. His sister's minister husband, who later dies in a plane crash, gets him into boarding school. He lives at the all boy boarding school. In summers he lives with friends. He's smart enough for college. His father would be proud. His father had no college. Princeton tuition is free if he does four years in the Air Force. "Once again we cheated death" whispers in his ear. He meets a small town beauty. He sits on her porch in the swing. Her pa spits into a cup. He has a girl named Kimberly because that's what you do. He doesn't know about family. Sit at the table. Eat your food. Say a prayer before it. His daughter is part of himself. A part that went to boarding school. A part that was yanked from his bed. Do it to him, do it. Thrown on the floor. Cheering. Do it to him, do it. Even teachers. Even them. But all that goes away. All that doesn't matter. There's books and thought and big ideas and philosophy to ponder. His daughter is a dream. A character in a book. She's not real. She's not a girl. She's a piece of him.*

"I still don't get the point of this." (Me in the dirt with the pencil.)

"I want to understand them."

Now I burst out laughing.

"There's nothing to understand." (Me.)

"Yeah, okay, but still."

She clicks the lighter into flame.

"Hey, what are you doing?" (Me.)

"Letting it go, letting it go

"That ritual's stupid, no."

She looks at the crumpled papers, now in the campfire circle, and I don't know if it's her or me but something changes her mind. I grab our parent's invisible hearts then race down the trail to the car. At the bottom of the trail, getting into the car, Kimberly rests for a moment before she turns the key. She drives us to the casita. When we pull up to the curb I start to hear the screams.

Chapter 33
Hunger

The screams are the Laughing Corpse. I find him splayed in the dungeon mind gripping the empty desk. He bellows like a bullfrog then presses himself to stand.

"What's happened to you?" (Me.)

"It's cold beneath my ribs." (Laughing Corpse.)

"Does it hurt?"

"Hurt?"

He's never once felt pain. I put my ear beneath his ribs and listen like a doctor.

"Tell me what's wrong. Tell me." (Laughing Corpse.)

"I think you might be hungry."

The Laughing Corpse drops his jaw.

"How can I be hungry?"

I don't have an answer so he flips into full on panic. He shakes his hands in front of my face to wiggle all his fingers.

"I can't pull my thumbs off. I scream whenever I try." (Laughing Corpse.)

"I think that's pain."

"Pain? Am I becoming human?"

He holds up the golden squirrel.

"The missing eye is back. Lava stones are loose. Throngs at the sacrifice ledge are full of your real real family. But, and here's the worst, none of them can see me. I'm ignored, walked through, completely disregarded."

"That does sound pretty human."

He lies on his back in silence, staring up at nothing. The light has left his bones. He looks gray. Lethargic.

"I feel hunger everywhere. It's not only under my ribs. I'm full of wants and wishes. It's me, me, me, everything is me. My viewpoint, my impression, my endless spewing judgment. I see your bloody leg and suddenly want to clean it. I see your tangled hair and suddenly want to comb it. I can't stay away from mirrors. I poke and prod and stretch myself and berate my own appearance. Where's my ukulele? Did I eat it?"

"No."

I pick up his ukulele from a pile of broken stones. He plucks the strings, desperate. I relax when I hear his voice. "Nobody likes me, everybody hates me, guess I'll go eat worms." I start to think he's back until he twangs and stops.

"My music sounds like rats."

"It's beautiful." (Me in truth.)

The Laughing Corpse holds his skull in the place where his ears would be.

"My ears are judging too! All of me is judging!" (Laughing Corpse.)

He springs away from the empty desk then hurls himself in the stones. I want to save him badly so I decide to comfort.

"You're not becoming human. You're made by me to love." (Me.)

"Liar. It's your writing. You're making me human

"That's not true

"Of course it is, of course

I don't have time to argue as I see the flat beret sliding down his skull. I put out my hands to catch it. It's now a gooey deflated thing and I stare at it in shock. So does the Laughing Corpse. We feel a heaving loss, a slam of broken love.

"See? You wrote it empty." (Laughing Corpse.)

"I didn't mean

"I know. Take it to Kimberly."

"Why?"

"To un-fear the invisible heart it must be held and kissed. Make her take it. Hold it. That might stop the death."

The Laughing Corpse touches his head, trying to look courageous. He rubs his hands on hatless bone as if it's a phantom limb. I carry the gooey deflated thing to Kimberly in the casita. She sits up and gasps when I enter.

"What's that?" (Kimberly.)

"You need to hold and kiss it."

"I'm not touching that. God, it even stinks. Get rid of it, it's disgusting."

"It's the old invisible heart."

"I don't care if it's caviar, I'm not letting it near me."

She grabs the invisible heart (holding it at a distance) and carries it outside. She pulls off the strap from the garbage can lid, holds the lid in her hand, plops the invisible heart inside then slams the lid on top. She struggles with the strap (it snaps her when she fastens) and curses the goddamn bears.

"I have to stop writing then." (Me.)

"Why? Why do you say that?"

"He's becoming human. He's all gray and dissatisfied."

"Well welcome to my world."

"That's not fair."

"Nothing's fair."

"Yeah but I don't want to kill him."

Kimberly looks at me now with a piercing gaze of need.

"Red Girl, please don't stop. Reading the words you write is revealing myself to myself. I'm someone I've never met and I'm still not in my life. I want to enter my life, live inside it, really live. If that means your Laughing Corpse has to become a human, well I'm okay with that."

She lifts the lid from the garbage can (unstrapping the bear strap first) to check the invisible heart. It's fallen under a greasy bag. When she moves the bag aside Lola and Wisp and Little One float up in the air.

"Why did you fly as ash?" (Kimberly to them.) "Why did Red Girl drop?"

"I'd like to answer that." (Me in a bit of a huff.)

"No, I'm asking them." (Kimberly to me.)

Little One goes first.

"Red Girl's very loyal." (Little One.)

"Much more loyal than us." (Wisp.)

Lola lights a cigarette. She inhales and exhales smoke as she looks at me, then Kimberly.

"I think" (Lola finally speaking) "It's because of the Laughing Corpse. He's really into control."

I start to go after Lola but I'm stopped by the racing dog. Kimberly hears his bark and turns away to look. He runs to her then sits. His tongue hangs out, panting. She pats him on the head while his tail slaps hard on the ground. Little One, Wisp and Lola slip away like clouds. When Kimberly turns to the garbage can she's left with only me.

Chapter 34
Death

"Do you believe Lola?" (Me in the casita.)

"I believe something holds you here and I want to know what it is."

Kimberly cleans her gin glass then starts a pot of coffee.

"I think you want to know too." (Kimberly.)

She's right. I do. I hate her.

"Go wherever the pencil goes." (Kimberly now with coffee.) "But do it fast, okay? We're running out of time."

I forgot about time. The casita has messed with our thinking and pulled us into a world. A world I thought was forever but is only a few more weeks.

"Then, if the bear is right, you can fly away for good." (Kimberly.)

Both of us glance away. We want our peace, the two of us, but we know it means goodbye. I press my pencil softy. It takes me to a death.

Year fifty-one. New York.

Kimberly no longer hopes to someday hear from our parents. She's burned the letters on the hill. She's moved through a divorce. She lives in a new apartment, still on the Upper West Side. She colors her hair. Creaks in one knee. Has written some plays she likes. She's starting one now at the wheelbarrow house (her ex-husband letting her use it) having just driven up tonight. She's opened her laptop, set out notes, then crashed on the bed for sleep. At 2 a.m. her iPhone rings.

"Mom?" (her younger son.)

He's on the home phone in the kitchen. The phone she used, years ago, to call our mother at Jim's.

"You got a voicemail here. It said your brother died."

"Did it say which brother?"

"No. But the woman had an accent."

"Wow. Okay, thanks."

"Sorry."

"It's right you called."

She hangs up the phone, mind racing. Her first thought is an accident. Car. Drunk driver. Boat. Her next thought is how to find out. She long ago deleted all the old family contacts. Their numbers are scribbled on paper, random shreds of paper, that are filed in various files, meaning shoved in a closet somewhere. She sits in the dark. The moon is out. She picks up the phone. Calls Tikko.

"Helumf?" (Tikko asleep.)

"Listen, I'm really sorry. I need to ask you a favor."

She tells him Jim has died. She doesn't know how or where and she'd like to call Maria. She hears some crashing from the phone as Tikko fumbles with boxes. They've been dating only a month, but Kimberly told him to stay at her place (from where he can walk to work) if he wanted to, and he did, so now he's wading through papers with Kimberly's voice in his ear. "Maybe in the shoebox." "Try that light green envelope." "Maybe the file marked 'old stuff.'"

With Maria's number (maybe) and Eliza's number (likely) Kimberly picks up the phone. Maria's rings and rings and doesn't go to voicemail. Eliza's rings and she answers, sounding thin and awake. She hasn't spoken with Kimberly for I don't know how many years, but her voice is open and matter of fact and they fall back into sisters. Eliza knows he's dead. She doesn't know what happened. Maria and Jim were moving, from Florida back to Maryland, so they're in a hotel, waiting to move, and Eliza has called the hotel. No one's there, no one knows, and Maria's cell doesn't answer. So that's where we're at. Shit. Yeah, it's pretty stressful.

Hours later Kimberly reaches Maria. Her cell had lost its power in the long long night before. She found Jim in the hotel room, after they'd moved some boxes. She'd stepped into the kitchen (it was a hotel suite) and when she came out he was blue. On the chair. Blue. She screamed and called 911. She pressed on his chest and prayed. But he was gone when the medics came and now she's back from the hospital, standing in the hotel room, her phone is charged, thank god, and her sister and brother will come, they'll come from Puerto Rico, will Kimberly tell Eliza? Heart attack? Sudden? She doesn't want to repeat this, she wants to lie down, wants to rest, tell Eliza, please, she really needs to rest.

"Eliza?" (Kimberly calling.)

They talk about what to do. Eliza and her husband can take two days off work. They can drive to Maryland. Eliza will call again.

When Eliza calls again the funeral is arranged.

"I'd like to go." (Kimberly.)

Eliza takes a breath.

"Yeah, okay. Yeah. Thing is, here's the thing. Mom and Dad aren't doing well and the stress might be too much."

"He's my brother."

"Yeah. I'm just trying to deal with them and it's hard to know

"I know. Tell them I'll be quiet. I won't talk or bring things up and it's all about Jim. Only Jim."

"Yeah, okay. Yeah. If you want to go down tomorrow, Maria would like you there. She told me to tell you that. The funeral's not for three more days so I'll talk to Mom and Dad and see if I can, I don't know, see if I can

"Thank you."

Tikko calls to tell her she shouldn't go alone. He's talked to the editorial desk (he's freelance at the Times) and he can take the week. They drive south on I-95 through the hottest day on record. In bumper-to-bumper they talk. He won't meet her family (no, that would be a mistake) but they'll find a hotel for several days and he'll stay put while she goes off to things they can't predict. Let's not even try. Let's not even think. Let's drive (Kimberly's driving) and watch for barreling trucks.

The suburb is dense with buildings but the brand new purchased condo sits on a woodsy river. Maria shows her the little dock that sticks out into the water. The river is why they loved the home and Jim was so excited, they were both excited, but now, well now, you never know, you never know what's next. They did an autopsy on him. The hospital said they had to, he was only fifty. It was electric, they said. An electric malfunction inside his heart so nothing to do. No warning. She's glad to have her faith. Jim was converting, did you know? Of course you wouldn't know, but he was going to be Catholic, converting very soon. You study with a group, and then you, oh, the phone. Maria picks up a cell phone.

"Cable on its way?" (Maria on the phone.) "Si, yes, okay."

She puts the phone on a counter once they're back inside.

"It's Jim's phone. Sorry. He set up the cable, everything for the move, so his phone keeps ringing and ringing and ah they're here. Come in."

Maria's brother and sister come in with the cable guy. They hold out friendly hands, sweaty in the heat. They've brought a container of coleslaw, some wings, some three-bean salad. They set out paper plates and the four of them try to eat. It's been a whirl. The heat is hard. Maria's brother and sister have to fly home for work. They can't stay for the funeral but they've been here this week. For that they're glad. Yes. Si. And glad to meet Jim's sister. Maria mentions our parents.

"They were here for several days and didn't show emotion. I don't think they can." (Maria.)

She looks to her brother and sister who hold up their forks in agreement.

"Maybe they're in shock. Or maybe they can't feel. Where do you get your feeling? You're so unlike your parents. I've said that, haven't I said that?"

The forks go up again.

"Tomorrow, if you'd like" (Maria to Kimberly only) "we're going to see the body. If you you don't want to go I'll understand, but Jimmy, your nephew Jimmy, is coming here tomorrow. He's Naval Academy, all grown up, we're going in the morning."

At the Hyatt on the highway (or maybe a Holiday Inn) Tikko sits in the lobby. He buys two gin and tonics while Kimberly fans her face. He tells some stupid jokes and Kimberly laughs and cries. She doesn't know what to do with the body thing tomorrow. Has he ever seen a body? She never has. Not laid out. It sounds scary maybe. Or maybe full and right. She'll go, she wants to go, Maria was kind to ask. At the little dock on the river Maria said something funny. Not funny haha but funny.

"Your mother, when we were alone, told me she believes you." (Maria at the dock.)

Tikko knows what happened during the un-forgetting. He knows what's funny but not haha in Maria's words at the dock. They shake their heads in the lobby. They'd both like another drink. When Tikko goes to the bar I start to get sad about Jim.

I tell the Laughing Corpse.

"He's my brother too." (Me to the Laughing Corpse.)

"You're right to be sad, you're right."

It's been a year since I fell as ash. The Laughing Corpse has cleaned my soot, swept the stones, dusted my sacrifice ledge. Now, with only me, he waits for a lift in our spirits. He keeps himself busy (we both do) but we miss the shyness of Little One, the calming voice of Wisp, the flurry of Lola's moods. We also miss Kimberly's life. I no longer really touch it. I have to hide as ash, burned, staying away. I can't make her cry or laugh or type out words on a laptop. She does this by herself now but misses me too, I hope.

"Do you think she does?" (Me.)

"Yes, of course she does!"

He throws me up in the air, taking me by surprise.

"You're so special Red Girl! Valiant! Loyal! Brave! You're the one who came back and for that you get more bones."

He picks up his ukulele and out falls a bag of silk. He holds the bag in his palms, presenting it like a crown.

"These aren't just any bones." (Laughing Corpse presenting.) "These are the bones of family. I gave them to Little One, Lola and Wisp but they left them behind in the burning. I collected them all for you. Saved them for an occasion."

I hold the bag of silk and shake out a thumb, an index, a little tiny pinky. I press them into my palm. Little One, Lola and Wisp are with me for a moment, a small imagined moment. Jim's there too, rowing, a welt on his sunburned shoulder.

Chapter 35
Cold Skin

Year fifty-one. Funeral home.

The cool forced air in the waiting room hits them with a blast.

"Oh that feels good." (Maria.)

The funeral man is tall and speaks with a swallowed murmur. He's practiced in front of a mirror, at least that's what I imagine, as Kimberly, Jimmy, Maria and a younger man with a clipboard follow him like tails. They stand in front of a solid door, knobs of brass, spotless. They can take as long as they like, the clipboard man will be waiting, he'll guide them back to the entryway, the place with the four upholstered chairs and vase of paper flowers.

"Should we go in together?" (Maria to Kimberly now.)

"The room is large. There's a couch." (Funeral man being helpful.)

Maria and Jimmy walk in first. Kimberly closes the door. She doesn't sit on the couch. She stands in the back of the room and watches Maria and Jimmy approach our brother Jim. Fake Jim. Joking Jim. Any minute he'll leap up and grab a fudgesicle oar. He's playing his part to perfection. All of them are. Even the lights. A spot is poised on the ceiling, sending a subtle beam, gentle and slightly pink, toward the face of faking it Jim. He lies on his back, looking up, surrounded by satin puff. There's muzak playing somewhere. A hint of lavender Glade. Kimberly watches Maria clutch her chest and moan. "Oh my god, he's cold!" Jimmy puts an arm out. He hugs her for a moment. A good performance, looking good, they're committing to the scene. Kimberly steps from the wall, pushing her hands together. Maria and Jimmy bow their heads. The back of their shoulders tremble as they whisper then pull apart.

"You can take a turn." (Maria wiping her eyes.)

Kimberly counts her steps as she walks herself to the coffin. She's not seen Jim for thirteen years. Maybe it's thirteen steps. At fifteen steps she stops. She lowers her head to look. Jim's face after thirteen years is still the face on the rowboat. But skin now plumped. Tinted. She sees the blue of his eyelids and all thoughts disappear. She's no longer watching a scene. She's watching Jim be dead. She holds her hand above him then lowers it to his forehead. The cold is damp and flat and shoves her into knowledge. He won't be grabbing an oar. He won't be leaping up. He'll do that in our mind or wherever memory goes but not on a lake in Maine, not with a welt to scratch. She stands in the silence of being dead. She sees herself outside, in a desert or a field, where she and Jim lie stretched on the ground for birds to swoop or bone pick. The sun shines dry and bright. It bleaches them with glory. They lie in a gift of nothing, a vast and empty space, with no horizon seen, no meaning sought or wanted.

She steps away from the coffin. She watches Maria and Jimmy. She leaves them alone, sits on the couch, as they stand again with Jim. Time expands then floats then settles into the satin. They nod their heads, quiet. They open the solid door. They follow the clipboard man to the place where you pay the bill.

Outside in the drenching heat Maria pulls out keys.

"Now we'll go to that place I like." (Maria in the car.)

Kimberly sits in the back and looks at Jimmy's head. It's shaped like her brother's head. She wonders what Jimmy knows of his father when he was young. She tells a few small stories. Jimmy turns to smile once, then goes quiet and still. Jim was quiet too. She looks out the window, rolling green, a haze that ripples trees. She doesn't know how to be. She doesn't know her brother's son. Doesn't know her brother. He's not the boy with an oar in his hand who one day caught an eel. He's the man with Maria and Jimmy.

At the Shrine Grotto of Our Lady of Lourdes they walk in the shade together. There's a boy of stone with a reaching hand. A grotto of holy water. A view of green below. Kimberly sits on a marble bench while Maria lights a votive. The votive is one of many, and as Kimberly watches Maria kneel she lets her mind untangle. It wanders through a life (I watch as hidden ash) of birth and youth and no more youth and many moments between.

It pauses in a pool. Maria out with Jimmy. Jim swirling his hand. "I swear I thought you were faking." The circle of water ripples, and Kimberly's pulled to an outer ring, far from the center, far, where she sees herself as a faker, a liar, a pretender. She sleepwalks in a hall, surrounded by a family, who knows/not knows and never says, never wakes her up, never lets her in on the secret joke she's living. Perception is constructed. It shifts like a moving cloud. Not a new idea, but one that hits Kimberly hard, sitting now on the marble bench, waiting for her cue, waiting to speak the lines that are written by someone else.

"I was in a play." (Kimberly to Tikko.) "Except when I touched his forehead. Something happened then and

She covers her face with her hands. They're sitting inside a Red Robin (or maybe a Ruby Tuesday) with burgers and fries on a plate.

"They don't even know I'm divorced." (Kimberly's face uncovered.) "Not that they need to, oh my god, there's enough going on right now. But Maria told me I'm lucky, 'be thankful you have your husband,' so it was strange to nod my head and smile like a fake."

"You're not a fake."

"I feel it. I feel it a lot, do you? Like I'm real/not real, I can't explain, I think it's from the family."

"I don't feel real/not real, but I can see why you could."

Tikko bites his burger. He chews it then sips his beer.

"In Japan I went to a funeral. I was teaching English, first year out of college. The bones go into an urn. Feet first. Neck last." (Tikko.)

"So you're not upside down?"

"Yeah."

"That's funny to me."

"I was hoping."

Chapter 36
Funeral

Year fifty-one. Next morning.

Kimberly watches our family mill around by the dock. Colin holds a paper cup. Eliza stands with our mother. Maria is near the water. Our father is near her arm. Kimberly freezes them there. Then she swoops her mouth up and steps inside the outline. Her laugh is a glass of champagne that shocks me with its sound.

Colin lifts his paper cup. "Whoa, you haven't changed!" Her laugh makes her light and sick. The family skirts like flitting bugs that Kimberly sees on the river, hovering over the water, landing on it, resting, sitting on top then flying. They talk about old dogs. Luke, Susie, fat 'ole Joe, the time, that time, when this and then. They touch the top of the river. "Damn that water's hot." They eat Dunkin' Donuts. They laugh at a piece of frosting stuck on Colin's cheek. Kimberly speaks with our mother. They stand beneath a willow, the two of them alone. "I know you did your best, Mom. I'm fine, okay? Know that. And email if you'd like." Our mother smiles, tears in her eyes. She'll never email, Kimberly knows, but she touches our mother's hair, brushing a tiny twig, and our mother lets her do it.

In the limo that comes to the condo Maria slips her a paper.

"Would you read this at the service?" (Maria.)

As she reads her voice is clear. She feels herself in the words. She's standing. Reading a prayer. Reading for Jim and no one else despite the tiny microphone and podium of wood. After she reads the prayer, Kimberly walks the aisle. She sits in a pew, next to the aisle, behind our mother talking. She's talking to a woman Kimberly doesn't know. "Yes, that's my oldest daughter. She lives in New York City."

A man at the podium speaks. He speaks of Jim and conversion, he was Jim's advisor, but Kimberly doesn't listen. Jim is in the coffin, covered now, waiting, circled by Jimmy, our father, and four young men in navy whites. Kimberly looks at Eliza, sitting next to our mother. Eliza rows and bails in the pew, as Kimberly, squinting, watching, sees her in Maine on the lake. She remembers the blur and ripple and remembers herself in light. Where Colin plays with a truck. Jim spools his fishline. Eliza, on the railing, sits on her saddle made from a towel as she trots or gallops through her fields, a stick in her hand, riding far, all the way to her edges. Kimberly holds them in a glass, a firefly, a flicker, as Jimmy walks up the aisle.

"I want to talk about family." (Jimmy at the podium.)

Jimmy speaks of family. The hope his father had that it could come together, hold itself in love. His voice is firm and real but as Kimberly listens in the pew she thinks about lies in a family. If everyone knows a lie is a lie it becomes a truth. She doesn't want that truth. Not for Jimmy or all the rest and yet she

"Okay, stop." (Kimberly in the casita.) "I don't want this funeral stuff. It's true, it's real, it happened, but the family never changed and this is not the way."

She runs some water in her hand and splashes it on her face.

"Yeah, I miss a group, roots, history, feelings, but not enough to deny you." (Kimberly.)

"Okay but

"We should be angry. Sitting in that pew, behind our mother, making nice, I know that underneath it all I had to be angry. Had to. I want to feel the anger. Get the stones."

"Oh no no

"It's time to try something else. I want catharsis, whatever that is, so get us really mad."

I jump to the dungeon mind. All the stones are gone. I check the empty desk. I climb up in the tree. I dig through Little One's closet then yell for the Laughing Corpse. He drags himself from the sacrifice ledge and I clench myself in shock. He's got skin on his bones. An eyeball in his head. The strings of the ukulele are snapped and hang like threads. The Laughing Corpse (looking bad) holds it under his arm.

"I need some lava stones." (Me trying to sound normal.)

"I ate them all."

"Oh."

"My hunger is out of control."

"But Kimberly wants our anger."

"Ah, so you're choosing her. I suppose I should have known."

I hold out my hand in comfort.

"No, don't touch me now. I'm not safe to touch." (Laughing Corpse.)

He looks at me in pain as he holds out the ukulele.

"There's one stone left inside." (Laughing Corpse.)

I take the ukulele and leave him looking bad. When I'm back in the casita I put it on the desk. Kimberly and I sit in a careful silence. Our anger could blow us up. It could send me away. It should (as we've been told) cathect and then empower. Kimberly has her fears (I have a few myself) but she wants to feel, wants to know, so here we are, choosing. Feel it. Feel it real. We're safe in the casita. It's her and me alone. No one else to scoff and laugh and tell us quit your whining.

Kimberly kisses my head.

"Just in case." (Kimberly.) "That's a kiss goodbye."

She shakes the ukulele until the stone drops out. It's the size of a fist. Kimberly picks it up then presses it to her chest.

Her heart begins to bang. Her skin begins to pop. Sparks of light and fire shoot inside her pupils. A surge of bright light spews. It hurts. It rips our body. It shreds every cell we have and every belief we hold. We're nothing but heat and rage and our muscles twitch and our body aches and it's too much, it's too much, we can't breathe, we're choking, but choking brings nothing but laughter, faces, frightening laughter, and we feel the back of our neck, a hand on the back of our neck, and the toilet water we swallowed, forced, we're forced to swallow, that's now coming up and out of our throats and we're choking on years and years ago, years and years and years. We shake and contort and shudder with sounds, the sounds of a madwoman angry, the sounds of a sane woman angry, the sounds of no, the sounds of rage, the sounds of a wrong occurring, the sounds of a wrong approaching, the sounds of protest against the world but the world is a place that holds it, the world is a place that loves it, the world is blind to wrong and right and only sees itself.

We collapse on the floor half dead. We wait to feel catharsis. After a long long silence Kimberly finally speaks.

"Are you still here?"

"Yeah."

"You feel any different?"

"Not really."

"Shit. Neither do I."

"Well, we tried."

"Yeah."

We laugh at ourselves from the floor until Kimberly shuts her eyes. I stay wide awake. While Kimberly drops to sleep I see a surprising thing. Our anger isn't finished. The stone rolls slowly on the floor and I see it grow as it rolls. A light pours in from the window. The light must be moon, not sun, as the morning is far away. A wind from nowhere (the door is shut) blows pages from the desk. I try to gather my pages but feel the tap of a paw. It's not the bear, I know it's not, the tap is much too soft. I push the pages aside and see the golden squirrel.

He's no longer gold. He's tin with yellow paint. I put him in my pocket (he's still a prize I won) then jump when I see the body. It's splayed out on the casita bed breathing with a snore. I creep up close to look. The body moves. I jump. I race to wake Kimberly up.

"There's a monster in here." (Me.)

My voice is high like a kid's. I clear my throat and try again.

"Kimberly. There's a monster."

Kimberly opens her eyes. I point to the body on the bed. She looks at it with a wary look, a hardness in her face. She lifts herself from the floor then walks up close to the body. She watches its rising chest then slaps her hand on its neck.

"Ow! What are you doing!" (The body.)

"Between you and I

"Between you and me. Me is an object pronoun. How could you make a mistake like that, how could you be so

"Stupid?"

The body looks at Kimberly.

"Oh no. Oh please. Am I   am I   no, please. Let me be someone else."

"You are what you are. Mine alone. That's all that can be said." (Kimberly.)

"No

"Then listen hard. Here's what I see when I look at you. I see a young man. Handsome. Brown eyes light and bright. You're tall. Strong. Friendly. Your smile is wide and open. Your laugh is deep and loud and it makes me feel, makes me know, that my jokes are the best jokes ever. You're the man I run to. You're the swinger-upper. You're the daddy I love. But I also see, I finally see, an ordinary prick. A dime-a-dozen man. A selfish jerk. A liar. A puffed up piece of pride. You might be someone else if you could only, if you would

"Anything." (Laughing Corpse.)

"Say to my face you're sorry."

"I'm very   I'm very   I'm very

He drops his head to his chest.

"I can't feel my conscience. I can't feel a thing. Where are my bones. Find my bones. I need to be re-made."

I race around the casita looking for some bones.

"Red Girl what are you doing?" (Kimberly.)

"He's not our father

"Yes he is

"No he's not our father

Kimberly swoops me up and puts me on his shoulders. I look at Kimberly down below then grip my hands in his hair. I feel the fear of falling while knowing that I won't. I feel my safety, feel my height, feel my thrill of him. I sit tall and proud, happy to be so happy.

"I love you Daddy." (Me.)

Kimberly gives me a look.

"Calling it love, calling it love, calling it calling it calling it." (Kimberly softly to me.)

I feel my body shake as Kimberly speaks again.

"I know it's hard, very hard. But you belong with me." (Kimberly.)

High on top of his shoulders I shudder with myself. I made the Laughing Corpse. He's real to me, so real. I feel the strength of his shoulders. I hear his quiet breath. The pulse of his missing heart beats now under my thighs. I'm calling it love, calling it love, calling it perfect love. I look at Kimberly watching. I see her patient face. She's standing in her life. She says I belong with her. I want her love, elusive love, a difficult love, not easy. High on top of his shoulders, holding his hair, gripping tight, something leaves my body. It slips away, slowly, languid as a snail. I'm blank, numb, tired, a child's empty skin.

"I can't re-make you." (Me to him.) "I no longer believe."

His body crumples to dust and I fall down in a heap. I sit in the dust. I'm a fool. I sift through his dust and find a rib. I press it in my hand. I breathe imagined love. I breathe imagined care.

"Help me help me." (Me.)

Kimberly touches the rib. She gently tries to take it but I hold on too tight. It breaks with a sound of crack.

"I'm sorry, Red Girl." (Kimberly.)

"I loved the Laughing Corpse."

Chapter 37
Morning

When morning finally comes I pick up all the pages strewn across the casita. I put them into order, straighten out the edges, give the pile to Kimberly who slides it in her backpack. I watch her pull down feathers, unscrew Walmart bulbs, wrap the aspen branch. I refuse to help. I'm still mad about last night when she killed the Laughing Corpse.

"We did that together." (Kimberly.)

"But you're the one who made me write."

"And I thank you for it, Red Girl."

"Why would you ever thank me?"

"You showed me something I couldn't know."

"That I'm a stupid dreamer? A crazy lying girl?"

Kimberly sighs and sits on the bed.

"His bones were loyalty love. Beautiful twisted loyalty love for a father we had to imagine. I've held a family of bones inside and never even knew."

She pairs the last of her socks then puts them in her suitcase. I try to jump to dungeon mind but there's nowhere to jump. My whole world is gone and I start to feel a panic. Kimberly's boring. Silent. I'm made for bigger things. I'm made to protect and save. I'm made to be very Oh. I'm made to

"Come on, let's go." (Kimberly.)

We're staying in Taos till Christmas Eve to see the Pueblo procession. Kimberly rented a room where I'm mad for another week. She tries to cheer me up.

"Look what I found in the suitcase." (Kimberly.)

She holds up Tikko's note.

"Solitude is right. Watch for bears in the mountains." (Kimberly reading the note.)

"Yeah? So?"

"Red Girl. If you don't want to fly away, you don't have to."

"Yes I do."

"It wasn't you that had to leave. It was the Laughing Corpse."

"I'm still not sticking around."

"Why?"

"You're boring without him."

Kimberly waits a moment. Then she sighs her sigh.

"I'm sorry to hear you say that. I feel great without him. I'm telling myself, and telling you now, that the loss of all his bones will lead to something else."

"Like what?"

"I've no idea. But I'm thinking it'll be good."

A few days later, Christmas Eve, we drive to the Taos Pueblo. The low sun reddens the sky and the

Mountain glows like an ember. Bonfires burn. Smoke curls up. The crowd is scattered and still. We hear the sound of gunshots. From the San Geronimo Chapel men walk out with a statue. They carry the Virgin Mary, making a winding loop, as we watch from near a bonfire. Little One, Wisp and Lola appear, dropping through the smoke.

"Leave the bones." (Lola.)

"Yes, she knows that now." (Kimberly.)

I step inside the fire. I float as a piece of char. I hover high and happy. I swirl and roll and twist and stretch myself like time. I'm a plinging rib. I'm a joke well told. Kimberly watches me fly and her thoughts rise up in bubbles. "Goodbye goodbye goodbye" and "Sayonara baby." I look at her down below. The top of her head has opened up and I see the crumbling ant farm, the tunnels I raced, the leaps I made, the strange little paths of brain. I wave goodbye to my home then press my ashy wings. I press and press against the sky until I shoot like a sparkler, a quick and crackling light.

Chapter 38
Home

Kimberly taps the steering wheel as she drives fast from Taos. She stops for a Snickers bar. When she walks back to the car I'm in the passenger seat.

"What the hell." (Kimberly.)

"Yeah I know I know

Kimberly laughs and laughs.

"Why are you back?"

"Got lonely."

"Well I would have missed you bad. You want to drive?"

I drive us well. We fly down the road like comets yelling wheeeeeee in the car. We'll stop in Amarillo, TX. We'll have Christmas dinner at Furr's Fresh Buffet. $12.95. All you can eat. We'll scarf three pieces of chocolate cake. We'll watch the groups of families, sitting crowded, piles on plates, forks lifting to mouths. We'll drive in silence for days. We'll think about the casita. We'll think about New York. We'll think about the pages piled in Kimberly's backpack. We'll finish the pages together. We'll read and redo and read. We won't fight or go crazy. We'll have an open window. We'll have a road before us. We'll have each other the rest of our lives no matter what we do.

"Amarillo's coming." (Kimberly seeing the exit.)

"I'm not blind."

"So get in the lane."

"I will I will

"It's coming fast

"Oh shut up and trust me."

###

A Checklist of JEF Titles

* Winners of the Kenneth Patchen Award for the Innovative Novel

- ☐ 0   *Projections* by Eckhard Gerdes
- ☐ 2   *Ring in a River* by Eckhard Gerdes
- ☐ 3   *The Darkness Starts Up Where You Stand* by Arthur Winfield Knight
- ☐ 4   *Belighted Fiction*
- ☐ 5   *Othello Blues* by Harold Jaffe
- ☐ 9   *Recto & Verso: A Work of Asemism and Pareidolia* by Dominic Ward & Eckhard Gerdes (Fridge Magnet Edition)
- ☐ 9B *Recto & Verso: A Work of Asemism and Pareidolia*by Dominic Ward & Eckhard Gerdes (Trade Edition)
- ☐ 11 *Sore Eel Cheese* by The Flakxus Group (Limited Edition of 25)
- ☐ 14 *Writing Pictures: Case Studies in Photographic Criticism 1983-2012* by James R. Hugunin
- ☐ 15 *Wreck and Ruin: Photography, Temporality, and World(Dis)order* by James R. Hugunin
- ☐ 17 *John Barth, Bearded Bards & Splitting Hairs*
- ☐ 18 *99 Waves* by Persis Gerdes
- ☐ 22 *The Chronicles of Michel du Jabot* by Eckhard Gerdes
- ☐ 23 *The Laugh that Laughs at the Laugh: Writing from and about the Pen Man, Raymond Federman*
- ☐ 24 *A-Way with it!: Contemporary Innovative Fiction*
- ☐ 28 *Paris 60* by Harold Jaffe
- ☐ 29 *The Literary Terrorism of Harold Jaffe*
- ☐ 33 *Apostrophe/Parenthesis* by Frederick Mark Kramer

JEF